Advance praise for *The Adventures of Nanny Piggins*, starring everyone's favorite flying pig!

"*The Adventures of Nanny Piggins* is the most exciting saga about a flying pig nanny ever told. There is a laugh on every page and a lesson in there somewhere. I recommend it highly."

—Madeleine K. Albright, former U.S. Secretary of State

"Like my favorite chocolate cake, Nanny Piggins is totally irresistible! This book is sweet, surprising, and makes me hungry for more. Delicious!"

—Peter Brown, *New York Times* bestselling author of *The Curious Garden*

"I like a title that tells you everything you need to know. I suppose to be really accurate they could have called this *The Funny and Surprising Adventures of Nanny Piggins (a Circus Pig in a Dress)*, but that's a bit long."

—Adam Rex, *New York Times* bestselling author of *Frankenstein Makes a Sandwich* and *The True Meaning of Smekday*

THE ADVENTURES OF NANNY PIGGINS

Best Wishes
R.A.Spratt

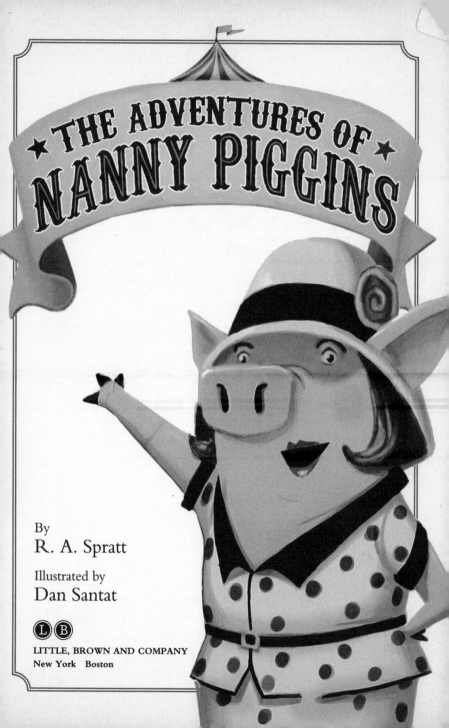

★ THE ADVENTURES OF ★
NANNY PIGGINS

By
R. A. Spratt

Illustrated by
Dan Santat

LB

LITTLE, BROWN AND COMPANY
New York Boston

Text Copyright © 2009 by R. A. Spratt
Illustrations Copyright © 2010 by Dan Santat

Little, Brown and Company

Hachette Book Group
237 Park Avenue, New York, NY 10017
Visit our website at www.lb-kids.com

Little, Brown and Company is a division of Hachette Book Group, Inc.
The Little, Brown name and logo are trademarks of Hachette Book Group, Inc.

The publisher is not responsible for websites (or their content) that are not owned by the publisher.

First U.S. Paperback Edition: June 2012
First U.S. Hardcover Edition: August 2010
First published in Australia in 2009 by Random House Australia Pty Ltd.

Library of Congress Cataloging-in-Publication Data

Spratt, R. A.
The adventures of Nanny Piggins / by R. A. Spratt ; illustrated by Dan Santat. —1st U.S. ed. p. cm.
Summary: When Mr. Green, a stingy widower with three children he cannot be bothered with, decides to find a nanny for his children, he winds up hiring a glamorous ex-circus pig who knows nothing about children but a lot about chocolate.
ISBN 978-0-316-06819-2 (hc) / ISBN 978-0-316-06818-5 (pb)
[1. Nannies—Fiction. 2. Brothers and sisters—Fiction. 3. Pigs—Fiction. 4. Humorous stories.] I. Santat, Dan, ill. II. Title.
PZ7.S72826Ad 2010 [Fic]—dc22

2009045047

10 9 8 7 6 5 4 3 2 1

RRD-C

Printed in the United States of America

Book design by Saho Fujii

DISCLAIMER

YOU ARE ABOUT TO READ A WONDERFUL BOOK. Nanny Piggins is the most amazing pig ever. It has been a privilege to write about her. But before you begin I must (because the publisher has forced me) give you one small warning....

Unless you are a pig, do not copy Nanny Piggins's diet IN ANY WAY.

You see, pigs and humans have very different bodies. Pigs are a different shape, for a start (mainly because they eat so much). Plus, Nanny Piggins is an elite athlete so she has a freakishly fast metabolism that can burn a lot of calories.

So please, for the good of your own health, **do not try to eat like Nanny Piggins**. There is no doubt that chocolate, cake, cookies, tarts, chocolate milk, sticky cream buns, candy, ice cream, lollipops, sherbet lemons, and chocolate chip pancakes are all delicious, but that does not mean you should eat them seven or eight times a day.

Also, you really must eat vegetables, no matter what Nanny Piggins might say to the contrary, or you will get sick.

Yours sincerely,
R. A. Spratt, the author

P.S. The publisher also wants me to mention that you really should not try a lot of the things Nanny Piggins does either. For example, throwing heavy things off roofs. Firstly, because you might give yourself a hernia lugging it up there. But mainly, because if it landed on someone that would be terrible. So please do not copy **Nanny Piggins's behavior** (unless you are under the close supervision of a responsible adult pig with advanced circus training).

To Angus

CONTENTS

CHAPTER ONE

Nanny Piggins and Her Dramatic Entrance

r. Green desperately needed to find a new nanny for his children. In the four weeks since their last nanny left, he found himself actually having to talk to them, provide them with meals, and pay attention to them himself. And all this just had to stop. He had a job at a law firm helping rich people avoid paying their taxes. He could not be expected to look after his children as well.

The reason Mrs. Green did not look after the children was because she was not there. Mr. Green said she had died in a boating accident. But the children were not entirely sure this was true. Yes, there had been a funeral. Yes, there had been an obituary in the paper. But people on television programs died all the time and that never stopped them from coming back in the next season. So they had not totally given up hope that their mother had just got fed up with their father, which was a sentiment they could fully understand.

There were three Green children. The eldest, Derrick, was a conscientious boy of eleven. Being older he was the natural leader. The only problem was he was never entirely sure where he was meant to be leading the others to, so he just kept a blank look on his face and hoped nobody noticed. He was always suntanned or muddy. Either way, he always looked brown. And he always had long messy hair but never went to the barber because the only time his father ever spoke to him was to snap, "Go and get your hair cut! You look like a scruffbag!"

The second child, Samantha, was a girl. And, as such, she had even fewer conversations with her father than Derrick. She was a nice nine-year-old and pretty enough, but not so much so as to cause a fuss. Her chief characteristic was that she worried all the time. To be fair, she did have a lot to worry about. Girls whose mothers have drowned in boating accidents would be foolish not to worry.

The third child, Michael, was only seven but, in many ways, he was the most confident. He could not remember his mother at all. So he was not saddened or worried about her loss. Derrick and Samantha bore the brunt of having to deal with Mr. Green. So Michael was able to get on with his life unhindered. As a result he was a little on the tubby side, because Michael's favorite hobby was stealing food from the kitchen, then sitting and eating it under a bush in the garden. Not that he was greedy, you understand. Because the fact is, most little boys would have this hobby, if only their mothers would let them.

On the whole they were three well-mannered, largely self-sufficient children. And they would have been a doddle for anyone to take care of. Mr. Green should have found a nanny in half a second flat. But there was a problem. Not only did Mr. Green believe that rich people should not pay taxes. He also believed that he, personally, should not have to pay for anything. He begrudged giving money to a nanny. In his opinion child care should be entirely government provided. Paid for out of the taxes his clients never paid.

But even more than that, Mr. Green deeply resented the idea that he had to pay to advertise for a nanny. There was so much unemployment in the world that, in his opinion, nannies should be beating down his door. So despite the fact that he desperately wanted a nanny, he did not have one because he was too cheap to put an advertisement in a newspaper. All Mr. Green had done was paint a sign himself with the words NANNY WANTED: ENQUIRE WITHIN, attach it to a stake, and bang it into the front lawn. So far the sign had sat there for three weeks without a single knock at the door.

And now the pressure was really on. One of the neighbors, having watched Michael sitting under a bush eating frozen pizza (that was still frozen), had reported this to the government. And a social worker had arrived to inspect all three children. She then made an appointment to see Mr. Green (because he was, of course, at work when she visited) and threatened him. She told him that if he continued to leave his children unattended for ten or twelve hours at a time, they would be taken away and put into government care.

Now Mr. Green would have liked nothing more than to be relieved of responsibility for his children. If that happened, then he would not have to go home at all. He could spend all his time at the office, happily reading tax laws. But Mr. Green knew that if his children were taken away from him it would look very bad indeed. (People did not think much of him already, what with him being a tax lawyer, and him not paying attention when his wife fell off the boat.) It would damage him professionally if the story got in the papers.

So it is at this point that our story begins.

Mr. Green was so desperate to hire a nanny, he was actually considering paying to advertise, when this painful thought was interrupted by a loud knock at the front door.

It was a dark and stormy night. Rain was pouring down. As Mr. Green opened the door he could not clearly see the person in front of him, silhouetted by the streetlight. But he could tell from the shape that the person was wearing a dress. So he assumed it was a woman. And he assumed she must have come about the position of nanny. Mr. Green was flooded with relief. "Come in, come in," he said.

As the new nanny stepped into the house, the light hit her, and Mr. Green could see her clearly for the first time. She wore a simple blue dress with a drop waist and a jaunty little jacket. And she was only four feet tall. But Mr. Green soon forgot about her lack of height when he saw that she had a much more shocking feature. The woman was not a woman. She was a pig. A common, pink farm pig. The type bacon came from.

"Good evening, I am Nanny Piggins," said Nanny Piggins the pig.

"Huh?" said Mr. Green.

"I have come to apply for the position of nanny," she explained.

"Well…" spluttered Mr. Green, buying time as his mind raced, and he tried to figure out what to do. "Well, um, that's very good. But, um… I wonder if you're quite suitable, you see."

"I can start immediately," said Nanny Piggins.

"Oh," said Mr. Green. He could not deny that this would be convenient.

"I have no criminal record," said Nanny Piggins.

"That is good," said Mr. Green. He could not deny that this would please the social worker.

As Mr. Green opened the door he could not clearly see the person in front of him, silhouetted by the streetlight.

"But I expect to be paid properly," stated Nanny Piggins.

"Now, that might be a difficulty," interrupted Mr. Green. Here he saw he had the perfect excuse for not hiring the pig.

"I charge ten cents an hour," Nanny Piggins declared boldly.

"You're hired!" exclaimed Mr. Green without even thinking. He knew a bargain when he heard one. "I'll be frank, Nanny Piggins, I would prefer not to have a pig take care of my children. But I am prepared to offer you the job until a suitable human nanny presents herself."

"Very well," said Nanny Piggins. "I think you will find human nannies are terribly overrated. They are, in my experience, very greedy and not terribly clean. But I shall agree to your terms, because it is wet outside and I do not have an umbrella."

So Mr. Green and Nanny Piggins shook hands on it.

Then Mr. Green immediately fled out of the house, to return to his office in the city, where he could read the tax laws in peace—leaving Nanny Piggins to acquaint herself with the children.

Derrick, Samantha, and Michael stared at Nanny

Piggins with their mouths agape. It had never occurred to them that their father might leave them in the care of a pig, no matter how well she was dressed.

"Hello, children, my name is Sarah Piggins and I am to be your new nanny."

"I'm Derrick," said Derrick.

"I'm Samantha," said Samantha.

"And I'm Michael," said Michael.

"Derrick, Samantha, and Michael. I shall try my best to remember that," Nanny Piggins assured them.

The children stared at her and she stared at them for several long moments before Nanny Piggins cleared her throat and asked, "So, what's supposed to happen now?"

"This is the part where you tell us what you expect of us," Derrick told her. He was quite an experienced hand, having had eleven different nannies in his time. (The nannies never lasted long because they could not bear working for Mr. Green. He was always forgetting to pay them and pretending to be deaf when they asked for food money.) So Derrick waited, expecting some boring lecture about the importance of cleaning behind your ears. But he was soon surprised.

"Oh, I didn't realize I was meant to have expectations

so early on. Give me a moment to think of some," said Nanny Piggins.

The children watched her as she thought for a few seconds.

"Okay, I'm ready," she announced. "Well, children, you need not tell your father this, but I will admit I have never been a nanny before. My only previous job experience was as a flying pig in a circus. Which, I am proud to say, I was very good at. And I don't suppose that nannying can be any harder than being blasted out of a cannon. So I shouldn't be surprised if I turn out to be very good at this too."

The children stared at Nanny Piggins in awe. They did not know what to think. They were astounded that she was a pig. But a flying pig? A flying pig who had no idea how to be a nanny? They must be the luckiest children in the world. Derrick was sure a flying pig would not be too vigilant about baths. Michael was sure a flying pig would not mind illicit frozen pizza being eaten underneath the azalea bush. And even Samantha started to worry slightly less, thinking a flying pig probably would not tell her off for all the incorrectly conjugated verbs in her French homework.

It was Nanny Piggins who interrupted their joyful thoughts. "So I've told you my expectations. What am I supposed to do next?" she asked.

The children considered all the things their father would have suggested.

"Well, you could tell us to go and tidy our rooms," suggested Derrick.

"Or instruct us to take a bath," added Samantha.

"Or order us to be quiet if we know what is good for us," said Michael.

"Oh, is that what you normally do?" asked Nanny Piggins, taken aback by the unpleasant suggestions. "Well, you can do that if you like. But I'm going to go to the kitchen and go through all the cupboards looking for things that contain sugar. Then eat as much as I can until I feel sick. You can join me if you like."

And they did.

The children soon fell deeply in love with their new nanny. And Nanny Piggins had barely shoved the first block of cooking chocolate in her mouth (then spat it back out because cooking chocolate does not contain sugar) before she fell in love with them too. They had a wonderful time together. She let them stay up half the night watching scary movies, then let them sleep in her bed the other half the night when they had terrible nightmares. She let them eat chocolate not only before and after breakfast but instead of breakfast as well. As far as they were concerned she was the best nanny ever in the entire world.

The only cloud on their horizon was the NANNY WANTED sign in the front garden.

For their father still held out the hope that he would eventually be able to upgrade to a human nanny. And the children lived in dread of that day.

CHAPTER TWO

Nanny Piggins and the Best Day Ever

anny Piggins was sitting at the breakfast table reading a rather thrilling romance novel. She encouraged all the children to read trashy literature at the dining table because it kept them quiet. And that kept Mr. Green happy. For Nanny Piggins had discovered that no matter what they might say to the contrary, adults like their children quiet, much more than they like them to have pure minds. She was just getting to a good bit (this is the best thing about a thrilling romance, there is a good bit on every page) when her daydream was interrupted by Mr. Green coughing. Not the cough of someone with an illness. But the cough of someone who wants to speak but does not know how to start. So Nanny Piggins stuck a slice of toast in her book to mark the page and waited to hear what he had to say.

"Nanny Piggins, I believe the children are due to start back at school tomorrow," said Mr. Green.

Nanny Piggins knew absolutely nothing about this, but she cunningly hid her ignorance with the guarded reply, "Yes."

"They'll be needing new uniforms and equipment, I suppose," he went on.

Again Nanny Piggins found herself wildly out of her depth. Being a pig, she had never attended school herself. So she had no idea how you needed to equip yourself. She cleverly encouraged Mr. Green to give more information by simply saying, "I suppose."

Mr. Green had obviously given a lot of thought to the next speech because it came out very suddenly and precisely. "Well, I'll give you five hundred dollars to sort it out. That ought to be enough, I should think." And with that he took a white envelope out of his suit pocket and placed it on the table.

All the children's eyes were fixed on the envelope, as indeed were Nanny Piggins's. This conversation was becoming stranger and stranger. She did not want to reveal her ignorance, but this was getting ridiculous. She needed to understand what was going on. "What is this?" she asked politely, nodding toward the envelope.

"The money, of course," said Mr. Green as he was getting up.

"Of course," agreed Nanny Piggins, pretending to be knowledgeable. Nodding her head as though she found it perfectly natural that Mr. Green should hide cash inside an envelope, as if it were too shameful to be seen by daylight.

"I will be home late tonight. I trust you will be all right with the children?" he said. Even though Mr. Green paid Nanny Piggins to be his nanny, he still could not entirely convince himself that she was willing to spend long periods of time with his children. He was relieved to hear Nanny Piggins's willing "Oh yes." It meant he could enjoy his dinner sitting at his desk, where it was quiet and peaceful and he could bill his time to a client as he ate.

Nanny Piggins and the children waited until they

heard Mr. Green close the front door behind him before they rushed into a huddle around the envelope. They all wanted to see the cash, so Nanny Piggins lovingly removed it from the envelope. The money was in the form of five crisp $100 notes. Nanny Piggins became quite misty-eyed, the notes were so beautiful to behold.

"All this money just to buy uniforms!" she exclaimed.

"Uniforms are ridiculously overpriced," explained Derrick. "They can charge what they like because they know you have to buy them."

"You do?" asked Nanny Piggins. This was news to her. "But what *are* these 'uny-forums' exactly?"

"Didn't you ever have to wear one in the circus?" asked Samantha, feeling both surprised and envious.

"I've never even heard of them before," Nanny Piggins assured her.

"They are horrible, uncomfortable clothes that you have to wear every day so that you match everybody else and nobody looks different," explained Michael.

"Oh." This was a concept Nanny Piggins understood. "You mean like costumes?"

"Sort of," agreed Samantha. "Except they are always

made in the dullest colors and the ugliest shapes, so that everyone looks as unattractive as possible."

"But why? Wouldn't it be better to look fabulous?" asked Nanny Piggins. That was certainly the object of all the costumes she had ever worn.

"Oh no," explained Michael. "People like children to look awful. Because it makes them pleased that they're not children anymore."

"It seems terribly cruel," Nanny Piggins muttered. Humans baffled her. They always talked about how they just wanted their children to be happy. Then they seemed to devise endless systems and schedules to ensure that they were not. The Green children had already suffered the loss of their mother, so to Nanny Piggins's mind, it was barbaric to force them to wear unfashionable clothes as well. "And you have to wear these uny-things to school?" Nanny Piggins asked. She was trying to get all this new information as straight in her head as possible.

"That's right," said Derrick.

Nanny Piggins could not hide the full extent of her ignorance any further. She had another question to ask. "So, what exactly is 'school'? Exactly."

"What's school?!" exclaimed Derrick. "Did you never have to go?"

He could not believe anybody as clearly knowledgeable about so many important things, such as how to make fake blood and what was the best type of stick for making a slingshot, could have had no formal education.

"No, you never *have* to do anything at the circus," explained Nanny Piggins. "That's the whole reason people run away there. To escape tyranny."

"So you could just eat chocolate? Every meal of the day?!" asked Michael, hardly believing his ears.

"Of course," said Nanny Piggins. "Many do. Particularly bearded ladies."

"Well, we *have* to go to school or we get in trouble," explained Samantha.

"Really? But how often do you have to go?" asked Nanny Piggins, imagining that it must be an institution used only for occasional punishment, only when children were caught being utterly wicked. Which could not include the three well-behaved Green children.

"We have to go every day," Michael told her.

"What! How monstrously cruel. Every single day?!" she exclaimed.

"Well, from Monday to Friday," Derrick admitted honestly.

"But still," exclaimed Nanny Piggins. "They force you to go! Even on sunny days when the weather is perfect for picnics?"

"Even then," the children regretfully assured her.

"And even on rainy days when the weather is perfect for going to the movies?" asked Nanny Piggins disbelievingly.

"Then too," the children added sadly.

"That sounds so terribly undemocratic," said Nanny Piggins. She was deeply shocked. "I thought we fought wars against dictators to prevent these sorts of things. Isn't this exactly why the French cut the heads off all their kings and queens?"

The children's knowledge of history was even less precise than Nanny Piggins's, but they were happy to agree with someone so sympathetic on this point. "We thought so."

"But who came up with such a mean-spirited idea?" asked Nanny Piggins. She was becoming increasingly horrified by the widely accepted brutality of universal education.

"The government," Derrick informed her.

"Of course, I might have known," said Nanny Piggins. "All the greatest psychopaths and evil villains end up in politics. If the government is behind it, I suppose there is nothing that can be done."

"I'm afraid not," agreed Derrick.

"They do seem to ruin everything," added Samantha.

"But still," said Nanny Piggins, thoughtfully eyeing the lovely cash on the table, "I find it hard to believe that it will cost a whole five hundred dollars to buy three uniforms."

"We need supplies too," Samantha reminded her. Samantha wanted a share in $500 pocket money as much as any sane girl. But she was also tremendously afraid of teachers, especially new teachers, and especially afraid of what a new teacher might say to a girl who had no pens or paper to write with.

"What sort of supplies?" asked Nanny Piggins absent-mindedly. Her brain was already turning over much more interesting possibilities for their newfound windfall.

"We need pens and notebooks," explained Samantha.

"And I need a geometry set," added Derrick. In truth, he had no idea whether he would be studying geometry or not. But he was sure that if Barry Nichols was in his class, he would like to have a compass. Just in case Barry got rough, and Derrick needed the sharp pointed instrument for self-defense as well as drawing circles.

"Yes, yes, we can get that later. But I'm sure the bulk of this can be invested in something more worthwhile," said Nanny Piggins. In her opinion there were more important matters to attend to. The three Green children needed fresh air and a good dose of fun, and she was just the pig for the job.

.... ★ ★ ★ ....

Happily, as it turned out, Nanny Piggins's idea of a good investment was to buy four tickets to an amusement park. The children had the most wonderful day. They went on all sorts of terrifying rides. On some they were flung high into the air until they were convinced they were going to die. And on others they were spun around and around until they were utterly sick.

In fact, Michael *was* sick. Fortunately the ride was going at full speed at the time, and the vomit flew cleanly out of his mouth and into the face of the person behind him. So Nanny Piggins did not have to trouble herself with cleaning up his clothes.

"Well done, Michael," Nanny Piggins complimented him. "With aim like that you could get a job at the circus."

And at lunchtime Nanny Piggins bought them lunch, right there in the park, even though the prices were ludicrously overblown. Nanny Piggins actually let them have hot dogs and hamburgers, and four cups of soft drink each. It was pure joy. Mr. Green would have dropped dead of apoplexy if he ever found out they did not take their own sandwiches.

It was a wonderful day. But, regrettably, this wonderfulness had come at a price. By midafternoon the $500 had been reduced to $89. Samantha had enjoyed the fun park every bit as much as the boys but, seeing the modest collections of notes and coins now stored in the dignity of the envelope, she was feeling the first symptoms of panic.

"I don't see how we can buy three uniforms for eighty-nine dollars," she worried. "Let alone supplies as well."

Nanny Piggins was busy savoring her third helping of cotton candy, and she was not going to let such practical concerns ruin her sugary bliss. "I'm sure we will think of something," she told Samantha optimistically. Then, remembering that she was the nanny and if she wanted to keep her job she had better not get the children into trouble, Nanny Piggins decided to get a sense of the enormity of the problem before her. "So what exactly does a uniform consist of?" she asked.

The apparently complete level of their nanny's ignorance was beginning to scare Samantha more and more. "Well, the boys must wear gray trousers and shirts."

This caught Nanny Piggins's attention. She sat bolt upright immediately. "But gray isn't Derrick's color at all!" argued Nanny Piggins, bewildered that neither the government nor the school had sense enough to realize this.

"That doesn't matter. All the boys have to wear the same," Michael explained.

"How brutal!" Nanny Piggins shuddered. "I'm almost afraid to ask what the girls are forced to wear."

"We have to wear a dark green tartan dress," said Samantha.

"Tartan? What? You mean you have to dress up as if you were Scottish?" Nanny Piggins asked disbelievingly.

"Well, yes," admitted Samantha.

"How very strange you humans are," said Nanny Piggins. "Nevertheless," she added bracingly, "I suppose we have to go along with it to keep your father happy."

"And the government from coming to get us," added Derrick.

"That too," agreed Nanny Piggins. "The less we upset the government, the better." She knew this from personal experience, but that is another story that will take up at least another whole chapter on its own. So we will not get sidetracked by it now. "Let's go to the shops. I'm sure I can easily put together some gray clothes and a Scottish dress and still have money left over for chocolate."

"You can?" Samantha was relieved to hear this.

"Oh yes," Nanny Piggins assured her. "They might not have forced me to go to school. But they did teach me a thing or two at the circus."

⋯⋯⋯⋯⋯⋯⋯⋯⋯⋯⋯ ★ ★ ★ ⋯⋯⋯⋯⋯⋯⋯⋯⋯⋯⋯

At the shop Nanny Piggins's eye was immediately drawn to a display of huge bars of milk chocolate. The bars were exactly like regular bars of chocolate except that they were enormous. This was an extremely attractive characteristic as far as Nanny Piggins was concerned. She and the children stood and looked at them for some time, occasionally picking them up to gauge just how heavy they were.

"Why don't we buy one?" suggested Michael.

"Hmm," said Nanny Piggins. She approved of this idea. Nanny Piggins could see that such large portions of chocolate had great potential. Like the amusement-park tickets, she felt the chocolate bars would make excellent investments. After all, she was supposed to be making lasagna for dinner. If the children had a pound of chocolate each beforehand, there was a good chance they would not want any dinner at all. Which would mean more time for television. After much consideration Nanny Piggins came to a decision.

"No, we will not buy one," said Nanny Piggins.

Michael's face fell.

"We'll buy four!" she declared, which made Michael grin happily.

"But what about our uniforms?" Derrick said. He too was beginning to have visions of angry teachers the next day. "The chocolate bars cost twelve dollars each."

"Yes, but they are on sale, reduced from fifteen dollars. So it would be a false economy not to buy them," Nanny Piggins argued.

"But then you would only have thirty-one dollars to buy three uniforms," said Samantha, as she quickly did sums in her head.

"And supplies," Derrick reminded her. Do not get them wrong. Derrick and Samanth both wanted the chocolate. But Nanny Piggins had only been their nanny for a short while, so they were still uncomfortable with being reckless.

"I'm the nanny. I make the decisions," said Nanny Piggins firmly. She was pulling rank because she could smell the chocolate through the wrapping. "Besides, thirty-one dollars is more than enough to make gray clothes and an ugly dress." And so she lifted four of the great big bars into her cart. "Now, let's get the supplies."

After a geometry set, three pens, and a twelve-pack of notebooks had been thrown into the cart, there were only nineteen dollars left of their budget.

"What are we going to do?" wailed Samantha. "We won't have anything to wear to school on Monday. It's just like in my nightmare. I'll have to wear my pajamas to class." Poor Samantha actually started crying.

Nanny Piggins gave her a hug. She did not like to see the children cry. It reminded her of all the upsetting events in her own life. Like the time she went three whole days without cake.

"There, there, it'll be all right. I'll think of something," said Nanny Piggins as she thoughtfully rubbed her snout. The children fell silent, genuinely hoping that their nanny's nose would hold a magical solution to their dilemma.

Seconds and then minutes stretched by, and Nanny Piggins still rubbed her nose. Just when Samantha was about to give up hope and curl up in a ball on the floor, Nanny Piggins suddenly shouted, "I've got it!"

"What?" asked Michael.

"Fetch me some gray dye and the ugliest dress in the store," ordered Nanny Piggins. The children had no idea what she had in mind, but they dutifully leaped into action. Derrick went to fetch the dye, while Michael and Samantha scurried off to look at women's clothes.

Later that night, after their three-course meal of chocolate, chocolate, and more chocolate, Nanny Piggins set to work making the uniforms. She took Michael and Derrick's best trousers and shirts and set them to soak in a tub of ugly gray liquid. The tan trousers and blue shirts quickly absorbed the dye.

Samantha's uniform was more tricky to mimic. They had not found an ugly green dress, but they had found an ugly and cheap pink one. The type of dress that cleaning ladies wear, that has a zipper up the front. At any rate, Nanny Piggins and the children then spent the rest of the evening converting it into a school uniform by coloring it in with wax crayons.

The tartan of Samantha's uniform was a complicated pattern of wide green and blue stripes highlighted with thin lines of white and yellow. Fortunately Derrick, Samantha, and Michael were all very gifted at coloring between the lines, so they made slow but steady progress. When they stopped for a chocolate break at eleven o'clock, three hours after good children usually go to bed, it was almost done. It looked so good, even Samantha stopped worrying. Although that may have had something to do with the fact that she was half mad from eating so much chocolate.

"Well, children. I think we have had an excellent day.

After their three-course meal of chocolate, chocolate, and more chocolate, Nanny Piggins set to work making the uniforms.

It is a shame your father does not give me five hundred dollars to buy uniforms more often," declared Nanny Piggins. The children only nodded their agreement, as their mouths were too stuffed full of chocolate to speak. "Let's have some more chocolate to celebrate!"

The next morning the children went to school. On close inspection, their uniforms did look slightly different. But the teachers did not notice. The homemade uniforms were ugly and, since they were just as ugly as all the other children's uniforms, there was nothing to make them stand out. This meant that Derrick, Samantha, and Michael passed through their morning lessons without comment. Apart from Barry Nichols, who said to Derrick, "Nice geometry set."

But sadly, at little lunch, things went terribly wrong. It was an extremely hot day. And, as it clearly says on the side of every box of wax crayons, "crayons should be stored out of the sun." And Samantha did not consider the full implications of this manufacturer's warning before agreeing to prove to Michelle Bampton that she was the world's greatest loser at handball. Five minutes into their grueling match, Samantha felt something trickle down her leg. At first she assumed it was sweat.

But when Michelle stopped playing midpoint to stare at her, Samantha looked down and realized her uniform was melting.

"Why is your dress going pink?" Michelle asked. For pink bits were indeed beginning to reappear, where the molten crayon had rubbed away. This was bad. Samantha knew she had to do something. But what? Her mind raced as she hastily tried to think of an exit strategy. She had barely asked herself the question, "What would Nanny Piggins do?" when the unnaturally deep voice of their deputy headmistress, Miss Bellows, boomed out behind her.

"What has happened to your uniform?"

Samantha felt like she was stuck in quicksand in a Tarzan movie. She was trapped and there was nothing she could do except hope that someone would come along to save her.

Meanwhile, the boys, oblivious to their sister's dilemma, had chosen to relieve the heat the way all thoughtless little boys do, by engaging in a water fight. To be fair, it was not their idea. They only decided to take part after Derrick had been hit in the head by a lunch box full of water. Within sixty seconds, they were both soaked to the skin.

Obviously, being wet is against school rules. But having dye run out of your school uniform and onto the school carpet and furniture is even more against the school rules, even if there is no actual rule stating that. And Derrick had a talent for making a mess in the best of circumstances. Giving him clothes made with cheap, hastily applied dye was, in hindsight, a recipe for disaster.

So Samantha was soon joined by Michael and Derrick, standing on a thick spread of newspaper outside Headmaster Pimplestock's office. And there they forlornly waited for Nanny Piggins to arrive.

Half an hour later Nanny Piggins strode in through the front door. Unlike the children, she looked fabulous. She was wearing a peppermint-green suit, which perfectly suited her pink complexion. And her hair was set into a series of elegant swirls miraculously balanced on top of her head. It looked as if it had taken three hours to arrange by a Hollywood hair and makeup artist. The children were used to seeing Nanny Piggins with chocolate smeared across her face, so they found it daunting to see her so immaculately groomed.

Nanny Piggins paused in front of Derrick, Samantha, and Michael and looked them up and down, clicking her tongue with disgust. Even though the whole thing had been her idea, she did look genuinely angry with them. The children hoped she was pretending. But, because she was so good at pretending, they could not be entirely sure.

Nanny Piggins marched into the headmaster's office. But before Headmaster Pimplestock could draw breath to voice his litany of complaints, she both shocked and pleased the children by unexpectedly yelling at him, "What on earth have you done to my children?"

"Done? Wh–Why…I…that is to say, the school…" spluttered Headmaster Pimplestock.

Nanny Piggins did not allow him to continue. "When they left home this morning, they were dressed in brand-new store-bought uniforms. Someone has obviously robbed them of their new clothes on their way to school. Perhaps within the grounds of this very institution."

"Madam, I assure you…" Headmaster Pimplestock began to protest. But Nanny Piggins was not going to let him continue.

"I am shocked that you allow this disgraceful crimi-nal activity to go on in a school. Mr. Green pays good money to have his children educated here, based on the assumption that they will be protected from crime. He will be most angry when I tell him about this. He will probably demand a refund of the fees," Nanny Piggins boldly declared. Now she really had Headmaster Pimplestock worried.

"My good lady, there's no need..." he began.

But Nanny Piggins interrupted again. "No need?! No need to ensure that Mr. Green's money is not wasted?"

"No, I mean no need to get upset. If the children's uniforms have been stolen by somebody, I'm sure not associated with this school, they can easily be replaced. We have a large supply of excellent-quality secondhand uni—"

"Secondhand! Mr. Green will not have his children wearing the secondhand hand-me-downs of strangers," declared Nanny Piggins.

"Of course. What I meant was that I am sure we, the school, can reimburse you for the cost of new uniforms," groveled Headmaster Pimplestock.

"That's more like it."

"Why don't you take the children home to bathe? Then, if they are fitted for their new uniforms tomorrow, we shall look forward to seeing them again first thing on

Wednesday morning...if that would be convenient for you?" Headmaster Pimplestock added, looking suitably browbeaten.

"All right," agreed Nanny Piggins.

Headmaster Pimplestock took the petty cash tin out of his desk. "Let's see, five hundred dollars ought to cover it."

The children could not believe it. Just when everything had gone absolutely, horribly wrong, when they were on the verge of being thrown out of school, disowned by their father, and probably thrown into a home for delinquent children, a miracle had occurred. They could not believe their eyes as they watched Headmaster Pimplestock count out another five crisp, new, $100 notes. Everything was going to be all right after all.

"Would you like it in an envelope?" Headmaster Pimplestock asked.

"Ah yes, to hide the money? Of course. No, on second thought, it's all right, I have my own," said Nanny Piggins, taking out her empty envelope from the previous day.

Five minutes later, the children and Nanny Piggins were walking out through the school gates. The children were still shell-shocked by their good fortune.

"I can't believe it! We've got the rest of today and all

of tomorrow off school," exclaimed Derrick. He was delighted.

"And we've got five hundred dollars to spend," said Nanny Piggins as she peered into the newly refilled envelope.

"But, Nanny, surely you should spend this five hundred on actually buying uniforms," said Samantha.

"Pish," said Nanny Piggins. "You don't need uniforms until Wednesday. I'm sure we can find something better to invest the money in in the meantime."

CHAPTER THREE

Leonardo da Piggins

Derrick, Samantha, and Michael charged into the room where Nanny Piggins sat, studying the television schedule and sipping her cup of coffee.

"Can Samson and Margaret come over to play?" asked Derrick, clearly struggling to contain his excitement.

"Please, Nanny Piggins, please," begged Michael.

Nanny Piggins pouted. She didn't like having her morning cup of coffee disturbed. Certainly not with the horrible suggestion of playing hostess to the Wallace children. "I really don't think they're suitable friends," she argued.

"We'll be really good," Samantha assured her.

"I don't know. Aren't there rooms that need to be tidied or things that need to be cleaned?" asked Nanny Piggins. She strained hard to think of an excuse, trying to remember the chores that she had heard little children should be expected to do. It is not that Nanny Piggins disliked the Wallace children. They were pleasant enough. As pleasant as rich children who never seem to dirty their clothes can be. What Nanny Piggins did not like was the Wallace nanny, Nanny Anne. Nanny Anne was just too disgustingly perfect to believe. She always wore perfect clothes and had perfect hair and arranged perfect day trips to perfectly complement the children's perfect education.

"Wouldn't you rather do anything else?" Nanny Piggins asked hopefully. "We could go mud wrestling, or throw things in the river to see if they float." These were two of Nanny Piggins's favorite activities. "Perhaps we could go mud wrestling and then jump in the river to see if we float?"

But the children were not to be outwitted. They were not very fond of the Wallace children either. They were, however, deeply in love with the remote control car that Samson (the oldest Wallace) had promised to bring. So they had devised a plan to tempt Nanny Piggins into agreement.

"Nanny Anne says she will bring a cake," said Samantha. All three children held their breath as they waited to see how their nanny reacted. Just as they expected, her ears immediately pricked up.

"What sort of cake?" Nanny Piggins asked cautiously.

"Samson is still on the phone. I could ask," suggested Derrick.

"Yes, run and ask him. I will need to know precisely what sort of cake before I agree to anything," Nanny Piggins said.

Derrick raced out of the room to the phone in the corridor. Samantha and Michael waited in silence with their fingers crossed. Moments later, Derrick burst back in. "Banana cake!" he wheezed. He was out of breath from the excitement and the running.

But Nanny Piggins pulled a face of disgust. "Banana cake," she said, managing to fit a lot of contempt into those two words. To her mind, cake and fruit were opposing forces. It was an insult to cake to try and combine the two. Admittedly, banana cake was not as bad as carrot cake. Grinding up vegetables and putting them in cake was, in her opinion, an act of fraud that should be punishable by imprisonment.

But Derrick had a trump card. "Banana cake...with chocolate chips!" he added triumphantly.

That sealed the deal. "Tell them to come at two o'clock," said Nanny Piggins.

"Hooray!" yelled all three children.

"Let's spend all morning making a really tough obstacle course to see if we can crash Samson's car," suggested Samantha.

"Good idea," agreed Derrick, and they rushed outside to do just that.

Nanny Piggins smiled fondly. Derrick, Samantha, and Michael really were such lovely children, she often forgot they were humans altogether and thought of them as pigs.

★ ★ ★

Later that afternoon, Nanny Piggins sat listening to Nanny Anne. It was a deeply unpleasant experience, a lot like having a fly caught in your eardrum: very loud and off-putting. But Nanny Piggins managed to bear the torment by making sure she had a slice of banana cake with chocolate chips in her mouth at all times.

"You seem to be enjoying the cake," simpered Nanny Anne with a smug little smile.

Nanny Piggins glanced at Nanny Anne out of the corner of her eye. She had indeed eaten three quarters of the cake on her own. And at such a speed that a considerable amount of it had become smeared around her mouth and across her face. But Nanny Piggins would sooner stick a pin in her hoof than admit she liked anything Nanny Anne had made. "Not enough chocolate chips," was her only response as she wedged yet another slice into her mouth.

Nanny Anne did not seem to mind being ignored. She was quite happy to sit and recite a monologue of all the worthy things she had done with Samson and Margaret. "I think it is ever so important to take children to the art gallery. They learn so much about beautiful things there. When was the last time you took your children to the art gallery?" Nanny Anne asked slyly, fully confident that whatever Nanny Piggins might answer, it would confirm her own nannying superiority.

Nanny Piggins might be feeling slightly ill from eating too much cake (no doubt it was the banana that was disagreeing with her), but she was not going to let herself be gazzumped by Nanny Anne. So she swallowed her large mouthful of cake and began to embroider the most spectacular tale her imagination could supply.

"I have been so busy teaching the children about the Westminster system of parliament, the role of the electron in the depletion of the ozone layer, and..."—she struggled to think of a third really impressive thing—"...and all about chocolate that I am afraid I have not had time to take them to the art gallery. It is on my list of the 3,700 incredibly important things I plan to do with them. The 3,521st thing was to go to the art gallery. And as it happens we did the 3,520th thing this morning, when I taught them how to light a fire with just a stick and a piece of string. So we will be going to the art gallery first thing tomorrow morning."

Nanny Anne was rendered temporarily speechless. Which, of course, had been Nanny Piggins's goal. Big fibs are much better than small fibs when you want to gazzump somebody. Nanny Piggins used the temporary silence to stuff the final piece of banana cake into her mouth and rudely say with her mouth full, "Thank you for coming but you had better go now, before we let the wild dog loose in the house for daily exercise."

"You let a wild dog exercise in the house?" asked Nanny Anne.

"Oh no, we let a wild dog in the house to exercise the children. It chases them around to keep them fit," explained Nanny Piggins.

Nanny Anne glared at Nanny Piggins beadily as she tried to assess whether or not she was telling the truth. But Nanny Piggins was a master of appearing to look innocent when she definitely was not. So Nanny Anne decided to gather up Samson and Margaret and make a hasty retreat without waiting to see the wild dog for herself.

.... ★ ★ ★ ....

"Did you enjoy playing with Samson's car?" Nanny Piggins asked her three hot and sweaty charges after the Wallaces were safely off the property.

"Oh yes," said Michael. "Derrick drove it straight into the fishpond. And Samson actually cried until he saw it drive straight up the bank on the other side."

"Well, I hope it was lots of fun," said Nanny Piggins, "to make up for the fact that now we all have to go to the art gallery tomorrow. Where we will, no doubt, be bored witless by millions of paintings of naked fat ladies."

"But why do we have to go to the art gallery?" asked Derrick, crestfallen to think that such a wonderful play-date had now gone so horribly wrong.

"It's all Nanny Anne's fault," explained Nanny Piggins. "The things I have to do to prove she's not better than me. It's ridiculous. I'll bet she's never been fired out of a cannon in her life. And still she goes around putting on airs."

"Will the art gallery be completely awful?" asked Michael. Until now his only experience of art had involved finger painting. Which, in his opinion, was wonderfully squishy and messy, but he suspected that grown-ups would know how to suck the fun out of even that.

"I imagine it will be utterly dreadful," said Nanny Piggins. But she relented when she saw the three sad faces. "Never mind. If we all wear sneakers, we can run around the gallery as quickly as we can. The whole thing shouldn't take more than five minutes. Then we can go somewhere else and eat ice cream." And this happy thought cheered the children up.

★ ★ ★

As it turned out the trip to the art gallery was not altogether unpleasant. There were a lot more violent bloodthirsty paintings than Nanny Piggins had expected, so she made the children stop running to have a look at them.

Derrick's favorite painting was of French soldiers charging into battle to kill Russians. Samantha's favorite painting was of a pretty lady called Judith chopping a man's head off with a knife. And Michael's favorite painting was of a field full of cows. The cows were not doing anything exciting but he had always liked cows, which was surprising, given that he did not at all like milk.

Fifteen minutes after entering the gallery, Nanny Piggins and the children made their way down to the final floor, having spent three times as long looking at paintings as they had planned to. Nanny Piggins was even beginning to think charitable thoughts like, "Perhaps culture isn't so bad after all," and "Maybe I'll bring the children back another day in four or five years' time" as they approached the final room. There was a sign by the doorway explaining that this final room did not contain works from the regular collection. These pictures were finalists in the gallery's annual portrait prize.

"What's a portrait?" asked Michael.

"Good question," said Nanny Piggins. This is what she always said when she did not know the answer to something.

"It's a painting of a person," said Derrick.

"Really?" asked Nanny Piggins. She was slightly impressed. Perhaps Derrick knew more about art than she realized.

"It says so on the wall," said Derrick, pointing to a sign on the wall.

"Ah, yes," said Nanny Piggins. "You can learn a lot from walls."

And so the four of them entered the room to see the portraits for themselves. Sadly, none of them liked what they saw. There were no soldiers, no beheadings, and not even any cows. But it was not the absence of these pleasant things that made the portraits so disappointing. The problem was they were all pictures of people and yet none of them looked like people at all. Some were done all with squares and triangles. And some were done with yellows and greens and other colors you would never see on a real person's face no matter how sick they were.

Nanny Piggins was horrified. She went over to the security guard standing in the corner. "What on earth do you call this?" she demanded as she pointed to a particularly unattractive blue stick figure of a man scratching his knee.

"That's what they call 'modern art,'" said the guard glumly. He clearly was not much more impressed himself.

"That's what *I* call a load of old rubbish," declared Nanny Piggins.

"You're not the first person to say that," admitted the guard.

"I could paint better than that with four hooves tied behind my back," said Nanny Piggins.

"You should give it a go then," said the guard. "These are the finalists from last year's competition. Entries for this year can be submitted up until next week...."

"I wouldn't waste my time—" began Nanny Piggins.

"The winner gets fifty thousand dollars," said the guard.

"What?" Nanny Piggins was electrified. "Did you say fifty dollars?"

"I said fifty thousand dollars," said the guard.

"Fifty thousand dollars! Why, that's more than five hundred dollars, and it's more than five thousand dollars!" Nanny Piggins tried to mentally come to terms with this enormous sum. "Surely that's more money than exists in the world?"

"Oh, it exists all right. And they give it away to any old nutbar who bangs down a bit of oil on canvas, if you ask me," said the guard.

"Well, I intend to be this year's nutbar," said Nanny Piggins.

.... ★ ★ ★ ....

Painting a portrait turned out to be a lot more difficult than Nanny Piggins had anticipated. She knew the actual painting part would be easy. All you had to do was wipe oil paint onto canvas in the right places. Any pig could do that. The hard part was deciding who to paint.

According to the rules of the competition the portrait had to be of "an important person." So Nanny Piggins and the children racked their minds all afternoon trying to think of somebody suitable.

"We must know someone important," said Nanny Piggins.

"I can't think of anyone off the top of my head," said Derrick.

"What about Headmaster Pimplestock from school?" asked Samantha.

"Yuck! Nobody likes headmasters," said Nanny Piggins dismissively. "They're always giving out punishments and reprimands. And they're almost always right, which only makes it worse."

"How about Hans the baker?" asked Michael.

"He's not important," Samantha pointed out.

"No, but he makes delicious custard tarts," protested Michael.

This weighed heavily with Nanny Piggins because she did like a custard tart almost as much as she liked a chocolate cake. But she suspected that the judges of the portrait prize would not share her high regard for the baking profession.

"No, we need someone who has really done something special with their lives: a hero, an adventurer, a really glamorous person," said Nanny Piggins.

"Then why don't you paint a picture of you?" suggested Michael.

"What?" asked Nanny Piggins.

"Oh yes, that's a very good idea. When you do a portrait of yourself, it's called a self-portrait. You could do one of those," said Samantha.

"Me?" said Nanny Piggins. She was not too sure.

"Of course, you're someone who has really done something. You've been blasted out of a cannon night after night at the circus," said Derrick.

"And there was the time they accidentally put too much gunpowder in the cannon, and you were blasted right through the roof of the tent. I bet no other pig has ever done that," added Samantha.

"And there was the time you made us triple-chocolate shortbread with chocolate-flavored cream," chimed in Michael. To his mind this was the one of the kindest acts ever, right up there with the complete life's work of Mother Teresa.

"True, true, very true," agreed Nanny Piggins.

"You have to be brave, heroic, and an all-around glamorous person to be blasted out of a cannon and be so brilliant at cooking," agreed Samantha.

"Everybody knows that," said Michael, even though the thought had never occurred to him before.

"You children all make good arguments," said Nanny Piggins. "I can see that I would make an excellent subject for a portrait. The only problem is, how am I going to paint myself? I can't sit across the other side of the room from myself to get a good look at my appearance. No matter how fast I ran back and forth across the room, I could never get far enough away from myself to have a really good look."

The logic in this really did stump the children. They thought long and hard on it for at least ten seconds before Samantha had the second brilliant idea of the day. "I know! You can look at yourself in a mirror," she said.

"Look at myself in a mirror," Nanny Piggins said, considering this idea. "Yes, I suppose that would work. The only problem would be that an image in a mirror is reversed, isn't it? So if I painted that, everything would be all backward. My left side would be on the right, and the right side would be on the left."

The children all looked at themselves in the mirror, poking first the left side of their faces, then the right side, and they realized she was correct.

"I know. We could cross our fingers and hope that none of the judges notice," suggested Derrick.

"That just might do the trick. After all, they were silly enough to like those paintings from last year, so it's not as if they are particularly clever people," said Nanny Piggins.

★ ★ ★

And so, that night, after a hearty dinner of caramel brownies and sherbet lemons (Mr. Green was away and Nanny Piggins was in charge of deciding the menu), Nanny Piggins set to work on her portrait. And the children stayed up to watch her, enthralled to see a masterpiece created before their very eyes.

As it turned out, Nanny Piggins was actually a very gifted painter. After all, you do not get top billing at a major traveling circus without having an artistic temperament. Just as Nanny Piggins had taken to being blasted out of a cannon the first time (she happened to be checking down

As it turned out, Nanny Piggins was
actually a very gifted painter.

the barrel of the cannon for cake at the exact moment they decided to test it), Nanny Piggins proved herself to be an accomplished painter on her first attempt.

It is hard to describe what any great masterpiece looks like. You really need to see it for yourself to appreciate the beauty of the brushwork, the composition, and the artist's use of color. But I will try to describe Nanny Piggins's self-portrait for you. Imagine Leonardo da Vinci's *Mona Lisa*, a mysterious, smiling woman dressed in black. Only instead of a human's face, imagine a pig's face. And instead of two folded human hands, imagine two folded pig hooves. Then you will have a perfect mental picture of Nanny Piggins's self-portrait. It was, in short, a breathtakingly brilliant artwork, the quality of which has not been seen since Leonardo da Vinci dropped dead in 1519.

Nanny Piggins proudly handed in her self-portrait, without a doubt in her mind that the fifty thousand dollars would soon be theirs.

The judges had three days to decide the winner. And they were a lovely three days for Nanny Piggins and the children. Each day they played a marvelous game called "What Shall We Spend the $50,000 On?" They all found this game endlessly entertaining because the more they thought about it, the more good ideas they came up with. Michael wanted to buy an elephant and ride it to school every day. Samantha wanted to buy a great big diamond, then shoot a laser through it to burn a hole in her math teacher's car. And Derrick wanted to buy a speedboat so he could quit school and become a pirate.

And so, before they knew it, they were being invited down to the gallery for the announcement of the prize. This was deemed to be such an important event by Nanny Piggins that she actually washed her face (using soap), even behind her ears, which destroyed several good smears of chocolate she had been saving for later.

There was quite a crowd gathered ready to hear the announcement. "You can tell which ones are the artists," Nanny Piggins said loudly, for she could be instructive when she chose to be. "They are the useless-looking ones wearing cardigans." There were indeed several useless-looking, grouchy young men wearing cardigans among the crowd. And those who had heard Nanny Piggins's comment glared at her instead of glaring meaningfully into empty space like they normally did.

But there was no time to consider their appalling dress sense because the director of the gallery was soon tapping the microphone and clearing his throat. Which is, supposedly, the polite way to say "Shut your trap" before beginning a speech. "Thank you all for coming..." the director started.

Nanny Piggins just rolled her eyes. "Get to the money!" she heckled.

The director of the gallery ignored her and warbled on. Nanny Piggins passed toffees out to each of the children to fortify them through the inevitable speechifying. Some time later, after thanking every one of his friends by name and making several simpering comments he mistook for jokes, the director did finally get to the point. "And now to announce the winner..." he said.

Nanny Piggins nudged each of the children to make sure they were paying attention. "But before I do..." he went on. Nanny Piggins and the children all groaned loudly. "...I have to announce that one of the entries, regrettably, had to be disqualified from the competition."

"Some twit didn't follow the rules," guessed Nanny Piggins.

"Unfortunately, we had to disqualify *Self-Portrait of a Flying Pig* by Sarah Piggins."

"Why?" shrieked Nanny Piggins, hardly believing her ears. At this point Samantha and Derrick actually had to grab their nanny to restrain her.

"Because portraits of pigs are not allowed in the competition," explained the director.

"But that's pigism," bellowed Nanny Piggins. She was really cross now. "How dare you stand up there and be piggist? In front of children too. You should be ashamed of yourself."

The director of the gallery was very taken aback. He had never been yelled at by a pig before. "I'm afraid there is nothing I can do. Samuel H. Wiseman, the founder of the Wiseman Portrait Prize, was very specific when he set down the rules."

The director took out a copy of the rule booklet and read from the first page: "Rule number one: The painting must be a portrait. Rule number two: The portrait must, under no circumstances whatsoever, be of a pig."

The whole crowd gasped.

"Why on earth would he write such a mean, beastly, prejudiced rule?" demanded Nanny Piggins.

"Well, I have done some research," the director admitted, "and according to his family records, he was apparently attacked by a crazed pig when he was a small child. He obviously held a grudge for the rest of his life."

"A man like that shouldn't be allowed to set up art prizes," Nanny Piggins said in disgust.

"I'm dreadfully sorry," said the director, before continuing with the rest of the prize-giving ceremony.

The portrait prize did indeed go to a horrible painting that looked nothing like anybody, let alone the person it was supposed to be. Unless it was meant to be a picture of a person whose head was caught in a vise and covered in orange paint. But Nanny Piggins had stopped listening. She had lost all interest in portrait prizes now that she was not going to be given one. It was such a shame, when they were all so terribly good at playing "What Shall We Spend the $50,000 On?"

The director droned on and on about "honor" and "the importance of art" and "prestige to the gallery," making Nanny Piggins wish she had brought some sponge cake to shove in her ears, but then he introduced someone Nanny Piggins did like. "Each year, as you know," said the director, "aside from the Wiseman Portrait Prize, which is, of course, judged by the finest art critics in the country, there is another prize."

Nanny Piggins's ears immediately pricked up.

"The security guards who stand in the gallery and look at the paintings all day long pick their own favorite. So now I'd like to introduce Guard Smith to announce the Guards' Prize."

Guard Smith approached the microphone. He was the same guard Nanny Piggins had spoken to a week earlier. And, thankfully, he had a much more direct style of speech-making than his employer. He cleared his throat and got right to it. "This year's Guards' Prize goes to Sarah Piggins, on the grounds that her painting actually looks like what it is meant to. And I know because I've met her and it's the spitting image."

Tears streamed down Nanny Piggins's face as she climbed up onstage to accept the award.

"Thank you, thank you so much," Nanny Piggins gushed. "It is good to know that there are still some people who truly appreciate real art."

"You're welcome," said the guard. "You certainly deserve it." And with that, he handed her the Guards' Prize—a large packet of chocolate cookies.

Nanny Piggins clutched the cookies to her chest. "What a wonderful, wonderful prize!" she exclaimed.

"I'm glad I didn't win the portrait prize now. I'd much rather have some chocolate cookies."

And they were really good cookies. The type that have to be stored in the refrigerator because there's so much chocolate in them. Not that Nanny Piggins's packet ever made it that far. She and the children sat down and ate them all on the spot. They then returned home, completely satisfied that they had beaten the art world at its own game.

CHAPTER FOUR

Mr. Green Asks a Small Favor (Then Immediately Regrets It)

I t was seven o'clock at night, and Nanny Piggins and the children were happily crouched on the floor of the cellar, holding a cockroach race, when they heard the distinctive *harrumph* sound of a throat being cleared behind them.

Now, one of the first things Nanny Piggins had taught the children was what to do if someone walks in on you when you are doing something bad. So the children did exactly as they had been trained—they stayed absolutely still and did not say a word, completely ignoring the four cockroaches as they scattered across the floor in front of them. Nanny Piggins made a mental note to recatch hers later because it was a big one with long legs and it would be a shame to let it run wild. Apart from making excellent racers, cockroaches can be tremendously handy for shocking hygienic people and clearing long lines at the deli. Nanny Piggins turned to see Mr. Green standing on the cellar steps immaculately dressed in a tuxedo.

"Um, Miss Piggins, I—um…how are you?" asked Mr. Green.

Nanny Piggins immediately knew he wanted something. Mr. Green never went to the trouble of remembering her name unless he really needed help. He usually never spoke to her at all. He just skulked in or out of the house without making eye contact. Nanny Piggins briefly considered running away, but then it occurred to her that Mr. Green wanting something could possibly be used to her advantage so, instead, she played along.

"I am very well, Mr. Green, and how are you?" she asked.

"Good, good, a touch of thrombosis, you know, but I can't complain," said Mr. Green, complaining. "I do, however, have a slight social difficulty."

"Oh dear," said Nanny Piggins. "Is it your teeth?"

"My teeth?"

"Nothing. Do go on," said Nanny Piggins.

"Yes, indeed," said Mr. Green. "You see, the thing is…" began Mr. Green again. For he was very bad at getting out information when he did not have the upper hand. As a lawyer, he almost always had the upper hand. He was usually either telling his clients off or telling other people off on behalf of his clients. He did not often have to ask for something, so he was not very good at it. "The thing is…" he repeated. Even though he was asking Nanny Piggins for something, it did not occur to him that it would be more polite not to waste her time. "…my law firm is having their annual dinner tonight."

"That's nice," said Nanny Piggins, although she secretly thought it would be the exact opposite. A room full of lawyers and lawyers' wives. She could not imagine anything more boring. As a former flying pig, conversations about managed funds and the best place to buy napkin rings were not Nanny Piggins's idea of excitement. And to have to eat dinner with such people would even take the pleasure out of the meal, which was really saying something because Nanny Piggins was a pig. So if you think how much you enjoy eating, then multiply that by a thousand, then add six, then multiply that by two, and then do not eat for a week so you will be really hungry, you will begin to appreciate how much pigs enjoy eating.

"The trouble is…" Mr. Green continued, "I was supposed to be going to this, er…dinner with Mrs. Havershaw."

"Oh dear." Nanny Piggins shuddered. "You poor man."

Mrs. Havershaw would have fit right in. Last time Mrs. Havershaw had cornered her, Nanny Piggins had thought she was going to slip into a coma. Mrs. Havershaw spent forty-five minutes droning on and on about her dahlias. It was fifteen minutes before Nanny Piggins realized dahlias were flowers.

"But she's just rung me and said that she can't come. Something about falling down a staircase and spraining both her ankles," explained Mr. Green.

"Really?" said Nanny Piggins. She secretly suspected that Mrs. Havershaw had come to her senses and thrown herself down that staircase, having decided that two sprained ankles was better than being bored to death by a bunch of lawyers.

"So I was wondering if you...um..." Mr. Green paused here, clearly hoping Nanny Piggins would add two and two together and realize what he was getting at. Nanny Piggins did realize what he was getting at, but she wanted him to say it himself because she enjoyed watching Mr. Green squirm.

"If I would sprain her wrists as well?" suggested Nanny Piggins. (Not that she would do this of course. But Nanny Piggins often said things like this to test Mr. Green to see if he was listening to her.)

"No, I was wondering if you would, in Mrs. Havershaw's place, be so good as to come with me to this, er... dinner," stammered Mr. Green awkwardly.

Now you have to understand, Mr. Green was already wearing his tuxedo, the carnation was already in his buttonhole, and it was already seven o'clock at night. He was clearly desperate. Nanny Piggins knew he had only hired her, a pig, to look after his children because he could not get anyone else. So to be asking her, a pig, to his firm's annual dinner, he was really scraping the bottom of the barrel.

"Don't do it," Samantha whispered to her out of the side of her mouth.

"Don't do it," Michael said, out the front of his.

Derrick was too horrified to speak. He just grabbed his beloved nanny by the elbow with the intention of never letting go.

Nanny Piggins did not need telling. She knew she did not want to go to the dinner. But she was interested to see to what lengths Mr. Green would go to change her mind.

"Who will mind the children?" Nanny Piggins asked.

"Mrs. Simpson from next door," said Mr. Green.

Nanny Piggins did not mind that arrangement. Mrs. Simpson was a good sort. She would bring marshmallows for the children. And she was too polite to enforce bedtimes.

"Acceptable," conceded Nanny Piggins. "But I am not accompanying you anywhere as an act of kindness. If you want me to go with you, you will have to make it worth my while."

She did not want to waste all night. If she was not going, she would rather get back to the activities she had planned with the children. After the cockroach races they were going to see who could spit a cherry pit the farthest. And Nanny Piggins had once spat a cherry pit ninety yards into a headwind, so she was keen to see if she could beat her own record.

"Well, I rather thought you would agree as a favor, a matter of kindness, you know…" said Mr. Green (he always took ten times longer than necessary to say the simplest things. It was a trick lawyers used to bore people senseless, then make them sign things they should not).

Nanny Piggins shook her head. "I don't think so."

"Yes, well, I can see that perhaps it would be better to make it an official business transaction," said Mr. Green, realizing that buying Nanny Piggins off was probably the simplest way out. "What would you like?"

"What are you prepared to give me?" asked Nanny Piggins as she tried to gauge how much she could gouge him for.

"I don't know. Flowers? Or maybe a new dress?" suggested Mr. Green.

Nanny Piggins wrinkled her snout. "You'll have to do better than that!"

"What do you mean?" asked Mr. Green. Nanny Piggins had him baffled. "Would you prefer cash? Or perhaps a savings bond?"

"Hah! You can't buy me off that easily," protested Nanny Piggins haughtily.

Mr. Green mopped his brow. He was beginning to be a bit frightened of his nanny. "Well, what is it you want?" he whined.

"I want an extra-large chocolate mud cake," said Nanny Piggins boldly. "Like the one in the window of the baker's shop."

"Is that all?" asked Mr. Green, considerably relieved.

"And I want written on top, in pink icing, *To Nanny Piggins, thank you so much. I am eternally grateful for everything you've done. Yours sincerely, Mr. Green.*"

"It would have to be extremely small writing," said Mr. Green.

"Or an extremely large cake," countered Nanny Piggins.

"Hmm...I see. I think I can arrange that," said Mr. Green.

"Then you've got a deal," said Nanny Piggins, holding out her hoof for Mr. Green to shake. "As soon as I've heard you ring the order through to the baker with your credit card number—and don't try giving him a false one because I have it memorized—I'll go and get changed."

She knew Mr. Green would have no scruples about trying to get out of his side of the deal. Being a lawyer, he was professionally required to be morally bankrupt.

.... ★ ★ ★ ....

Mr. Green had never understood why it took women so long to get dressed. That is because he was a very silly man of limited imagination. Applying makeup is essentially painting on your face. And it would be foolish to rush painting on your face, especially when you are going out to an important dinner.

Nanny Piggins was an accomplished show business performer, so she knew that getting dressed was not a matter to be taken lightly. She was in the bathroom for a good hour and a half, using heating devices on her hair and applying a variety of creams, powders, and pastes to her face in exactly the right quantities.

Meanwhile, Mr. Green waited at the bottom of the stairs having a nervous breakdown. The dinner was supposed to start at eight o'clock. And he was already half an hour late. You have to understand, Mr. Green was fifty-one years old, and he had never been late to anything before. Apart from when his wife was giving birth to Derrick and he promised to be there to be supportive. He was nine hours late that day. But he'd had an emergency at the office. There had been a jam in the photocopier—his arm. You see, Mr. Green was not a very mechanically minded man, and when he reached into the photocopier to change the toner, his cuff link became snagged on the drum wheel. As a result, the fire department had to be called to set him free, and by the time he got to the hospital he was already the father of a bouncing baby Derrick. But Mr. Green prided himself that he had never been late for anything important, that is, work related.

He preferred to turn up to everything early so he could say "tut-tut" and look meaningfully at his watch when other people were late, or even just on time. So he had no idea how his bosses were going to respond to his being late for the company dinner. He just hoped they would not respond by firing him, or the only punishment worse than firing him, firing his secretary and forcing him to make his own cups of tea.

When he heard his children yelling, "She's coming, she's coming!" he was already transported to a state of euphoria, even before he looked up to see the amazing vision of loveliness at the top of the stairs.

You do not get fired out of a cannon for years without learning a thing or two about catching the eye. Nanny Piggins knew how to make herself a sight to behold. She wore a long, flowing, silver sequined gown that seemed to reflect back every light in the house tenfold. She also looked taller, partly because her hair was painstakingly coiffured perpendicular to her head in every direction. And partly because she was wearing a dozen long peacock feathers strapped in a band around her scalp.

And some mention must be made of her face, because it was truly impressive. She had blotted out every trace of her natural features using pig-toned makeup and then redrawn all her features so that they looked slightly prettier than they had looked before. The effect was disconcerting and yet attractive.

Mr. Green had never seen a more beautiful-looking pig. "Why, Nanny Piggins, you look..." He was lost for words.

"You look beautiful," Samantha told her. When it came to compliments, she was much more articulate than her father.

"I know," agreed Nanny Piggins. "Beauty has been a lifelong burden of mine. Even butchers sigh when I pass, but that's beside the point. You three are going to have the house to yourselves all evening. So be sure you make good use of the time. I expect the house to be a mess and at least one piece of furniture to be broken by the time we get back. And if you are not still awake when we get home I shall be bitterly disappointed in you all. So enjoy yourselves and have as much fun as possible while we're gone." With that, Mrs. Simpson arrived, so Nanny Piggins kissed Derrick, Samantha, and Michael good-bye before disappearing into the night with their father.

"Do you think she will be all right?" Samantha asked Derrick.

"She'll be all right. It's Father who's in for it," said Derrick, because, when all was said and done, he was the oldest and the wisest.

★ ★ ★

By the time they got to the dinner, Mr. Green and Nanny Piggins were one hour and five minutes late. And yet Mr. Green still paused before entering the banquet hall to give

Nanny Piggins last-minute instructions on how to behave. "Now, er ... Miss Piggins," he said, "there will be some very important people present at this dinner this evening."

Nanny Piggins just rolled her eyes.

"The senior partners for example shall all be in attendance. Isabella Dunkhurst in particular is a woman who is — how can I put this — frightening. So you had best not talk to her. Or indeed anyone. If you could remain completely silent for the next three hours that would probably be the best approach," concluded Mr. Green.

"The deal was that I got the mud cake if I came. You didn't say anything about me having to behave," said Nanny Piggins.

"Well, I thought that was obviously an implied part of the deal," began Mr. Green.

"Tsk-tsk, Mr. Green," said Nanny Piggins, for she could drag things out when she wanted to as well. "A lawyer should know better than to assume something is implied. You should have included it in the small print of our deal. It's too late now." With that Nanny Piggins turned on the flashing fairy lights in her headdress, brushed past Mr. Green, and walked into the banquet hall. She was too hungry to stand around getting lessons in manners.

The dinner did not go at all as Mr. Green had planned. Nanny Piggins was completely silent for the first fifteen minutes as she wolfed down all five courses of the meal. Both her own and Mr. Green's servings. He was too horrified to be able to eat anything. Then she immediately set to work making friends.

It turned out there was something much worse than Nanny Piggins upsetting Isabella Dunkhurst. And that was Nanny Piggins and Ms. Dunkhurst becoming buddies. Nanny Piggins struck up the friendship by challenging the veteran lawyer to a drinking contest. Having downed a bottle of lemonade in a quarter of Ms. Dunkhurst's time, Nanny Piggins proceeded to teach her new friend "Issy" to tap-dance on the head table. The rest of the evening was a blur.

Within half an hour of their arrival, Nanny Piggins had all the assembled lawyers up on their feet and dancing with her. These were people who had never before danced in their lives. Even as three-year-olds they had

Nanny Piggins proceeded to teach her new friend "Issy" to tap-dance on the head table.

refused to do the hokeypokey because they did not want to look undignified.

Mr. Green tried to keep up with Nanny Piggins because he did not want to look like a bad sport. Particularly when all the senior partners obviously thought she was tremendously good fun. The problem was that it's hard not to look like a bad sport when you are a bad sport. Mr. Green got separated from the party when they were en route to a disco and Nanny Piggins demanded that the taxi stop so they could go paddling in the park's duck pond.

Mr. Green had gotten out of the taxi and was trying to be a joiner. But it took him so long to get his shoes and socks off that his colleagues were splashing off into the darkness before he had even rolled up one trouser leg. He sat on his own, waiting for them to return, but when they still had not come back an hour later, he rolled down his trousers, put his shoes and socks back on, got in a taxi, and went home.

There he sat and waited in his study, dreading to think of the damage to his career Nanny Piggins would cause.

He must have fallen asleep at some stage because he was woken up at eight o'clock the next morning by the smell of fried eggs and hash browns. He ventured out into the kitchen to discover Derrick and Samantha cooking breakfast as Nanny Piggins, still wearing her dress from the night before, regaled the children with the story of her adventures.

"...and then I climbed up the flagpole with his wet trousers and hung them from the top. So we must all go down to the town hall after breakfast to see if Senator FitzGibbon's pants are still there, because I promised to get them down once they were dry."

Mr. Green cleared his throat. This was his favorite way of calling attention to himself. It saved him having to think of something to say.

Nanny Piggins and the children turned to look at him.

"So you had a good evening then?" Mr. Green asked. He knew he had to find out what went on but he was not sure where to begin.

"We had a pretty good night," said Nanny Piggins cautiously. "For a bunch of old fuddy-duddies, they warmed up all right."

"Good, good," said Mr. Green, although he clearly thought it was nothing of the kind. "So, er..." He was trying to get to the important bit that he really wanted to know. "So, er…nobody said anything about, er…firing me for taking a pig to the annual dinner then?"

"Nobody said anything about you all evening," said Nanny Piggins conclusively, as she bit into a delicious egg sandwich.

Now many people would have taken this as an insult, but it is a testament to how boring Mr. Green is that he found this to be a great relief indeed.

"Oh good," he said. "Well, I'll pop out and pick up that cake for you, shall I?"

"That would be very nice," agreed Nanny Piggins between mouthfuls, "although you might want to get me two cakes while you're there."

"Why?" asked Mr. Green. He could never see why he should part with any more money than he had to.

"Because Ms. Dunkhurst offered me a job," said Nanny Piggins. "She wants me to be the new senior partner. She thinks it will be a refreshing change to have a partner who has never studied law."

"Oh my gosh!" exclaimed Mr. Green. He clutched his chest, desperately wishing that he would be struck dead with a heart attack then and there.

"Sooo..." said Nanny Piggins, letting him wallow in agony for as long as possible, "I thought you might want to bribe me not to take the job."

Mr. Green sighed a huge sigh of relief. "Two cakes it is then."

With that he rushed out of the house and down to the baker's before she could increase her demands.

CHAPTER FIVE

Nanny
vs.
Nanny

The Green children were sitting on top of their family home learning about Newton's law of universal gravitation by throwing things off the roof. The whole thing had been their nanny's idea. She knew a lot about gravity, being a former flying pig. They had started with apples and bags of flour, and progressed to potted plants and their father's portable radio. The children were impressed to discover that even though he was old and dead, Isaac Newton really knew what he was talking about.[1]

Samantha did worry about hitting people. But Nanny Piggins assured her that while it was wrong for normal people to throw things off roofs, it was all right for her to do it because she was the world's greatest flying pig and therefore had impeccable aim.

Nanny Piggins was just about to throw Mr. Green's filing cabinet off the roof when Michael noticed a woman standing at the front of their house.

"Who's that?" he asked.

Derrick, Samantha, and Nanny Piggins peered over the edge to have a look. It is hard to tell a lot about someone from the top of their head. All they could see was her broad-brimmed straw hat, the swaying material of her long skirt, and the large guitar case she held in her hand.

"Do you think she is some kind of traveling musician?" asked Samantha.

"Just because someone has a guitar case does not necessarily mean she has a guitar," said Nanny Piggins. "In

---

[1] Now readers, you must not do this at home. Not only will you get in trouble. You will also get Nanny Piggins in trouble. And where there is trouble there is always less chocolate; it is just one of those cruel facts of life.

the olden days mobsters used to carry weapons in violin cases. So imagine the contraband you could get into a guitar case—they're much bigger."

They all lay with their noses just over the edge of the roof wondering about just that, when the woman actually had the audacity to look up at them.

"Quick, hide!" said Nanny Piggins.

There was no reason for them to hide. This was their house. If anybody had a right to be up on the roof, throwing things off, it was them.

"Hello, you people hiding on the roof," called the hat-wearing lady. "I've come about the Nanny Wanted sign."

"She's a nanny?!" exclaimed Samantha.

"Who wants your job!" yelped Michael.

"What should we do?" panicked Derrick.

"I wish we hadn't thrown everything off the roof already or we could have dropped something on her," said Nanny Piggins.

"We've still got the filing cabinet," Michael pointed out.

Nanny Piggins looked at the filing cabinet. It was the heavy four-drawer variety. "We'd better not. We'd probably get in trouble if we hurt her."

They all peered over the edge of the roof again. The

"We'd better not. We'd probably get in
trouble if we hurt her."

hat-wearing lady had short blond hair, piercing blue eyes, and the ugliest gray dress in the world. She was looking at the NANNY WANTED sign on the front lawn. It was impressive she could read it. The sign had been out in the weather for so long, black mold now covered several of the letters.

"She doesn't look like a psychopath," ventured Michael.

"Psychopaths never do. That's why they're so dangerous," said Nanny Piggins.

"Don't worry, I'll handle it," said Derrick. Then leaning forward and yelling in a clear voice, he said, "Go away, please. We already have a nanny!"

Nanny Piggins got a little teary. She was very fond of the children. It touched her heart to know they were fond enough of her to yell at a complete stranger.

But then the worst possible thing happened. Just as the hat-wearing woman started to turn away, Mr. Green's car pulled up, and Mr. Green got out.

From up on the roof they could not hear what he was saying. But they knew he was gushing and sucking up, because Mr. Green always did that when he was talking to blond women. It was a mental weakness of his. They watched as Mr. Green led the hat-wearing woman into the house.

"Bottom!" said Nanny Piggins, which just shows how strongly she felt because she rarely swore. "We'd better get down there and nip this in the bud."

Nanny Piggins and the children edged across the roof gable, shimmied down the guttering, and crawled back in through the upstairs bathroom window as fast as they could. By the time they got down to the living room, the hat-wearing woman and Mr. Green were having a cup of tea and a cookie.

"Ah, Miss Piggins," said Mr. Green as Nanny Piggins and the children entered the room. This was already a bad sign. Mr. Green usually addressed Nanny Piggins as Nanny Piggins. The fact that he had already dropped her job title showed that he was about to drop her job as well. "This is Nanny Alison. She has been a professional nanny for ten years and has excellent references."

"Really?" said Nanny Piggins. She could not think of anything more lengthy to say. Her mind was too busy hating Nanny Alison.

"You can't get rid of Nanny Piggins, you just can't," protested Samantha.

"Samantha, what have I told you?" demanded Mr. Green.

"That I should be seen, and not heard, until I turn eighteen. When I can say 'Good-bye, I'm returning my key' before moving out of home," chanted Samantha.

"Precisely. It is not your business to interfere in the hiring and firing of domestic staff," said Mr. Green. "When Miss Piggins came to us, it was on the strict understanding that she would be replaced with a suitable human nanny when one became available. Isn't that right, Miss Piggins?"

Nanny Piggins just squinted at Mr. Green. She was not listening to what he was saying. She was thinking about biting his leg.

"But surely you want to make sure you employ the best nanny possible," said Derrick. "What will people say if they think you have hired a second-rate nanny?" Derrick knew his father hated to think people were talking about him.

"You should test her," suggested Michael, knowing he personally hated being tested, and hoping this alone would be enough to put Nanny Alison off.

"I suppose we should have some kind of test of nannying skills," said Mr. Green.

"I have no objections to a test. Rigorous competitive examinations are a healthy process both for the subject and the examiner," said Nanny Alison.

Nanny Piggins and the children just stared at her. They were not quite sure what she had said, and they definitely had no idea why she had said it.

"All right then," declared Mr. Green. "We'll have a series of tests starting tomorrow morning at seven o'clock sharp."

★ ★ ★

Unfortunately, the next morning Nanny Piggins woke up at ten past eight because somehow during the night her alarm clock had been smashed into 214 pieces on the floor. Nanny Piggins dressed hastily so she could undo any damage Nanny Alison had caused while she was oversleeping. But when she tried to leave the room, the doorknob was missing.

"That's strange," said Nanny Piggins to herself. "I'm sure that doorknob was there when I closed the door last night." But there was no time to think; Nanny Piggins needed to get downstairs. So she climbed out the window, shimmied down the drainpipe, snuck around the back of the house, and came in through the back door.

When she found the family, they were just sitting down to breakfast in the dining room. "Ah, Miss Piggins, glad you could join us," said Mr. Green. (This is another example of an adult saying the opposite of what they mean.)

"Where have you been?" whispered Derrick.

"There must have been an earthquake in the middle of the night—my alarm clock got smashed. Have I missed anything?"

"In the hour before breakfast Nanny Alison taught us to sing in three-part harmony," said Samantha.

"You poor, poor children," said Nanny Piggins, sympathizing deeply.

At that moment Nanny Alison glided into the room carrying breakfast. Nanny Piggins glared at her in dislike. When Nanny Piggins came out of the kitchen she always had smears of whatever she had been cooking all down her front and sometimes down her back as well.

Nanny Alison looked like she had been Scotchgarded. There was not a mark or a wrinkle on her.

"What have we got here?" asked Mr. Green as he hungrily eyed the food.

Nanny Alison set a plate in front of him. "For you, sausages and hash browns. A little bird told me they're your favorite."

"I told her," protested Michael, who did not like being referred to as a little bird.

Nanny Piggins glowered at Mr. Green. She did not approve of him eating sausages, and he knew it.

"And for the children," continued Nanny Alison, "seventeen different types of boiled vegetables." She set the three plates of gray sludge in front of them. "Little ones need their fiber to keep them regular," explained Nanny Alison.

"Just so, just so," said Mr. Green. Adults often repeat themselves when something is not worth saying even once.

Michael looked like he was about to cry as he dug his fork into the tasteless gray glop.

Nanny Piggins had had enough. "I am going to go into

the kitchen to make myself some chocolate pancakes," she declared. Apart from wanting to eat them herself, she could sneak some out to the children. But as she reached for the kitchen doorknob the strangest thing happened. She missed, because the doorknob was not there.

"Where's the doorknob?" she asked.

"No time for that," said Mr. Green as he finished his meal and wiped the sausage fat off his face. "We need to get on with the test. The second round of the Nanny Games is laundry."

"Hang on, what was the first round?" protested Nanny Piggins.

"Cooking breakfast," said Mr. Green. "You lost that one because you weren't even there."

Nanny Piggins glared at Nanny Alison again. She was beginning to suspect that perhaps there had not been an earthquake, and in fact something else had caused her alarm clock to break.

"You each have a basket full of dirty clothes. The task is to clean these clothes as quickly and efficiently as possible," said Mr. Green.

"But that's easy. We can both just put them in the washing machine," said Nanny Piggins.

"I have disabled the washing machine," revealed Mr. Green, holding up a large mechanical doo-dah. "You have the option of trying to fix the washing machine. Or you can wash them by hand. It's up to you."

"What a stupid test," said Nanny Piggins glumly. Because even though it was stupid she could not see how she was going to get out of it.

"Come on, Nanny Piggins," encouraged Samantha. "You have to win. You're already one point behind and we don't want Nanny Alison to be our nanny. Apart from cooking vegetables for breakfast, I think she might be evil."

"There's no doubt in my mind," Nanny Piggins informed her.

"On your marks...get set...go!" called Mr. Green.

Nanny Alison whipped up the laundry basket and dashed into the kitchen. Straightaway they heard the tap go on as she began hand washing. Meanwhile, Nanny Piggins stood and stared for a moment. Then she too whisked the laundry up and started running. The difference was Nanny Piggins did not run for the nearest sink. She ran for the front door, down the front path, and into the street.

"Do you think she's running away from home?" asked Samantha as they watched her disappear around the corner.

"No. She wouldn't take our dirty laundry if she was," Derrick reasoned.

Nanny Alison worked her way through her basket of laundry like a machine. Her arms never seemed to get tired of scrubbing. Mr. Green was clearly impressed. He obviously had visions of selling his actual washing machine if he hired her. After fifty-three minutes she only had the socks to go, and they were the easiest to wash because they were so small. There were eight socks in the basket, and the children counted them down helplessly. It looked like Nanny Piggins was about to lose the second test as well.

When, suddenly, Nanny Piggins burst in through the back door.

"Finished!" she shrieked as she raced into the room and dumped her basket on the kitchen table. Not only was the laundry shining bright and clean, it had also been dried.

"How did you manage that?" asked Samantha in amazement.

"You know that retired army colonel who lives around the corner?" said Nanny Piggins.

"The one who's deeply in love with you?" asked Michael.

"That's the one. I nipped around to his house and threw it in his machine. We had seven chocolate cookies and a lovely chat while it went though. He's even got one of these new washing machines that is a dryer as well," said Nanny Piggins.

Nanny Alison was just washing out her last sock. "Finished," she declared.

"Well done, you both took about the same time," said Mr. Green. He was really determined not to be impressed by Nanny Piggins's ingenuity.

"Yes, but Nanny Piggins got her washing dry as well," protested Derrick. "That has to count for extra points. It's ready to wear." As he said this, Derrick took out his school sweater and put it on to demonstrate. Unfortunately he was not able to get it over his head. "I must have picked up Michael's accidentally." Derrick dug through the washing basket and found the other boy's sweater. He held it up against himself, and it was immediately apparent this was not his either. It was even smaller. It was doll sized.

"Oh, Nanny Piggins," said Samantha holding a hand over her mouth in horror, "you've shrunk everything."

"What?" said Nanny Piggins. "But I had to put everything on super-mega-extra hot to get it dry in time."

"The point goes, once again, to Nanny Alison," declared Mr. Green.

And so the rest of the morning went on. Nanny Piggins lost the Vegetable Peeling, Gutter Cleaning, and Long Division Explaining tests as well. She got caught telling Michael, "Don't bother to learn that. Long division is a waste of brain space, when you can just buy a calculator." Which is only the truth.

The Games were suspended while they all took a break for lunch. They ate a compote Nanny Alison had whipped up by cooking the flavor out of twenty-six different types of fruit.

"There's something not right about her," Nanny Piggins muttered darkly as she handed cookies to the children under the table. "It's not natural to be that good at being a nanny," said Nanny Piggins. "She needs to be investigated."

"But how?" asked Samantha.

"You distract her while I sneak upstairs and search her room," suggested Nanny Piggins.

So, as Michael pretended to have smallpox by drawing pink dots on himself with a felt-tip pen, Nanny Piggins slid to the floor and crawled across the room and out the window, then up the drainpipe and into Nanny Alison's room.

Nanny Alison's room looked nothing like Nanny Piggins's room. There were no circus posters, no dusty knick knacks, and no clothes strewn about every surface. Her neat little suitcase sat neatly on the floor. And her neat guitar case lay neatly on the bed.

Nanny Piggins tried the suitcase first. It proved to be very disappointing. All it contained was one clean dress, six sets of clean underwear, and a big, thick instructional manual entitled *How to Raise Children Properly*. Nanny Piggins briefly flicked through the book. It had chapter headings such as "The Pros and Cons of Beating," "When to Lock a Child in the Cellar," and "The Medicinal Benefits of Cod Liver Oil." Nanny Piggins tossed the book aside and turned to the guitar case. It was fastened with a large combination lock. This struck Nanny Piggins as unusual. In her experience, guitarists usually wanted to be able to open their guitar cases as quickly as possible, so they could bore people with folk songs at the slightest provocation.

To a normal person this large combination lock would be very hard to break open. But Nanny Piggins happened to have a pair of industrial-strength bolt cutters in her pocket so she easily demolished the lock in half a second. But when she flipped open the lid she could not believe what she saw.

The guitar case was absolutely chock-full of doorknobs. Doorknobs of all different shapes and sizes and colors and textures. Some were old, some were new, some were shiny, and some were dull. They had obviously come from dozens of different buildings. And in the middle lay the plain brass doorknob from Nanny Piggins's own bedroom. "Nanny Alison is a doorknob thief!" exclaimed Nanny Piggins. She raced downstairs to tell the children.

Nanny Alison was in the middle of providing after-lunch entertainment in the form of a marionette puppet show. Mr. Green thought it was fabulous, mainly because it was free. It did not even need electricity.

The children were bored witless until they heard Nanny Piggins's news. "Why on earth would anyone want to steal doorknobs?" asked Derrick.

"It is probably a form of mental illness," suggested Nanny Piggins.

"How are we going to catch her out?" asked Michael, because he had read a lot of detective novels so he knew catching people red-handed was the best way to solve a crime.

"I've thought of that," said Nanny Piggins. "And the answer is, superglue!" Nanny Piggins held out a tiny tube to show them.

"What will that do?" asked Samantha.

"We'll put it on all the doorknobs. Then when Nanny Alison tries to steal one she will stick to it and we will have caught her red-handed," explained Nanny Piggins. The children liked the sound of this plan. They helped Nanny Piggins, each taking it in turns to sneak about the house, smearing glue on doorknobs, while Mr. Green laughed a little bit too loudly at the marionette puppet show.

"Right," said Mr. Green. "We'd better get on with the Nanny Games. Although Nanny Alison is already winning five points to zero. You only have to lose one more point, Miss Piggins, and that is it. I'm afraid you'll be looking for a new job." Again, Mr. Green was not really afraid of this. He was feeling the exact opposite.

Mr. Green cleared his throat and read from his notebook, "For the sixth round the nannies will be required to..." But Mr. Green never got to reveal what the sixth round was because at that moment Samantha triumphantly screamed, "Aha!"

"What?!" asked Mr. Green, bewildered.

"Nanny Alison was trying to steal the doorknob. Look, she's stuck to it!" declared Samantha. And, indeed, Nanny Alison was unable to remove her hand from the living room doorknob.

"That proves she was trying to steal it," declared Derrick.

"What are you talking about, you stupid boy?" said Mr. Green. "It only suggests that she was trying to open the door."

And so Mr. Green's mediocre legal mind had found a flaw in Nanny Piggins's brilliant plan. Opening doors was a perfectly legitimate reason for touching doorknobs.

"Why on earth would anyone want to steal a door-knob?" asked Mr. Green incredulously.

"Mental illness," suggested Michael helpfully.

"Who gave you such a stupid idea?" asked Mr. Green. The children gave Nanny Piggins away by looking everywhere but at her.

"I might have guessed," said Mr. Green, puffing out his chest, ready for a good long rant. "Not only are you a second-rate nanny and a pig, you also have the audacity to slander the name of Nanny Alison."

Fortunately Nanny Piggins was saved the trouble of having to slap Mr. Green hard across the face, because at that exact moment a police detective kicked the door in and burst into the room.

"What on earth is going on? How dare you!" blustered Mr. Green.

"Sorry, sir," said the police detective. "We would have used the doorknobs except there aren't any." Turning to Nanny Alison, he continued. "I am arresting you for Grand Theft Doorknobs." Then, much to Nanny Piggins's and the children's delight, he snapped a pair of handcuffs on Nanny Alison. (Which was not easy given that her hand was still superglued to the living room doorknob. But an oxyacetylene blowtorch soon fixed that.)

But even better than that was the sight of Nanny Alison screaming wildly as four policemen dragged her away. "Nooooo! I haven't found it yet. Don't put me away without letting me see it. Please, please!" But she was no match for four burly young constables and they soon bundled her into the waiting van.

The police detective explained. Nanny Alison had been traveling about and posing as a nanny so she could steal doorknobs from all the finest houses in the country. As Nanny Piggins had correctly suspected, Nanny Alison had the mental illness doorknobitis.

"But how did you know to find her here?" asked Samantha.

"She was bound to come here. Because all doorknobbers (this is what people who collect doorknobs are called) know this is the home of the most famous doorknob in the world."

"It is?" said Derrick, Samantha, and Michael in perfect unison. Their three-part harmony lesson had still not entirely worn off.

"This is the home of the late Edith Green, the famous professor of antiquities, isn't it?" asked the detective.

"That was our mother," said Derrick.

"I didn't know she was famous," added Michael.

"Oh yes, because she discovered the legendary Fabergé doorknob. And attached it to a door in this very house," said the police detective.

"No!" said the children, again in perfect unison.

"It's true." Mr. Green sobbed with shame.

The children and Nanny Piggins had forgotten he was there. They preferred to think about him as little as possible.

"If you would be so kind as to show it to me, sir, just to confirm that it is unharmed?" asked the police detective.

Mr. Green slowly led the way into his study and over to the bookcase full of law books. He was weeping softly. "I never wanted her to bring it into the house. Nineteenth-century Russian décor is so gaudy."

"Just show us the knob please, sir," said the policeman.

Then to the surprise of all, Mr. Green put his hand on a small marble bust of Ronald Trout (the inventor of the goods and service tax) and the entire bookcase slid to one side, revealing a small, ornately carved wooden door. But they barely noticed it because there, in the middle of the door, was the most spectacularly beautiful doorknob ever made. It was decorated with gold filigree and exquisite enamel work, and studded with diamonds, emeralds, and rubies.

"This was your mother's secret room," explained Mr. Green.

"That is the most amazing doorknob ever!" exclaimed Derrick.

"Which is why Nanny Alison wanted to steal it," explained the police detective.

But Nanny Piggins's mind was working on a different track. "Tell me," she said. "If this beautifully carved door, with the most beautiful doorknob ever, is so cleverly hidden...then what I want to know is—what is behind the door?"

Mr. Green started to sob louder. "Your mother's great weakness."

The children looked at one another.

"She was your mother. One of you had better open it," said Nanny Piggins gently.

Derrick stepped forward because he was the eldest. And if his mother kept a live tiger behind the door, it was only right he should try to fight it first. He reached for the Fabergé doorknob and turned it carefully. The latch clicked back and the door swung out toward him. There, inside the room, was the most amazing sight. A huge pile of chocolate. There was white chocolate, milk chocolate, dark chocolate, fruit-flavored chocolate, and chocolate-flavored chocolate from all the different countries in the world.

"Your mother was a chocolate collector. She earned her PhD in chocolate. Her life's dream was to put together the most comprehensive chocolate collection in all the world," explained Mr. Green. He could barely get the words out, he was so mortified.

"What a wonderful woman," marveled Nanny Piggins as she looked up at the towering stacks of chocolate. "Well, there's only one thing for it. As a tribute to your mother's memory, we owe it to her to eat as much chocolate as physically possible."

"But won't that ruin her collection?" asked Samantha.

"Not at all," declared Nanny Piggins. "It will still be the world's most comprehensive collection of chocolate bar wrappers. And it would be morally wrong to let all this chocolate go to waste."

The children were not going to argue with that. So Nanny Piggins, the children, and the police detective all sat down to enjoy the chocolate and fondly remember Mrs. Green, the great professor of antiquities and collector of chocolate. And as they sat in her hidden chocolate storage room, the children felt a little less sad about how much they missed hugging her.

CHAPTER SIX

Nanny Piggins and the Great Voyage

Brilliant ideas often came to Nanny Piggins when she was asleep. To be strictly accurate, they came to her when she was awake, lying in bed with her eyes closed, not wanting to get up yet. Either way, bed was a place of creative genius for her. And so it happened on this particular day, as she snuggled beneath her comforter, that Nanny Piggins was struck with wonderful inspiration.

She shook Derrick, Samantha, and Michael awake. All three of them were asleep on Nanny Piggins's bed because they enjoyed sleeping in too. And they knew Nanny Piggins's room was the only place their father would not harass them about it. Mr. Green never entered his nanny's room because (even though he would never admit it) he was slightly afraid of her.

"Wake up!" cried Nanny Piggins. "We've got no time to waste."

"What's going on?" asked Derrick.

"Is the house on fire again?" asked Samantha.

"I don't think so. That's not why we have to get up," urged Nanny Piggins. "We have to get up because I've had a brilliant idea."

The children immediately perked up. Nanny Piggins's brilliant ideas were always much more brilliant than anybody else's.

"What is it?" asked Michael. "Have you figured out how we can try space travel after all?"

"No, not that," admitted Nanny Piggins. "Although I have been thinking about it. No, I've had an idea about what we can do in the meantime."

"What?" asked all three children.

With Nanny Piggins, anything was possible.

She might suggest building a catapult, or entering a tango competition, or selling one of their father's law degrees so they could have some money to go to the arcade.

"Let's go to the beach!" declared Nanny Piggins.

This was a surprising suggestion. It was five years since the Green children had been to the beach. They assumed their father did not want to take them because it reminded him of their mother's tragic boating accident. In truth he did not take them because he was too cheap to pay for three children's bus tickets, and he did not like the effect the sea breeze had upon his hair.

Even though, strictly speaking, the children would not classify going to the beach as a "brilliant" idea, it was definitely a wonderful idea to them. And they also knew from experience that Nanny Piggins had a talent for turning even ordinary ideas into brilliant realities.

Nanny Piggins and the children looked quite a sight on the bus because they had so much luggage. Nanny Piggins did not believe in leaving things to chance. She insisted on bringing anything that could possibly be necessary to ensure a wonderful day at the beach, which, to her mind, involved a lot of equipment. They had two large suitcases full of gardening implements for building sand castles, binoculars for invading the privacy of other beachgoers, peashooters for tormenting annoying people, and plenty of cakes and lemonade to sustain them (just in case all the shops at the seaside were shut because everyone in the area had simultaneously caught a cold).

The Greens lived a long way from the coast. Mr. Green did not like being close to nature. Seeing things bigger and more powerful than himself, like the ocean, made him feel that he was not quite in control. Which was, of course, true. But he did not like to be reminded of it.

The bus journey was long and windy. The children were wedged between the suitcases, which jolted into them every time the bus turned a corner. But they did not notice their discomfort because they were enjoying looking out the window so much. Of course, looking out a window can be dull. But not when you have someone like Nanny Piggins giving you a running commentary.

"Look at that woman's head!" Nanny Piggins exclaimed.

"It's a wonder she has the courage to go out in public. I'd strap a cat to my head before I'd leave the house with hair that color. And look at that man's trousers! There's nothing to hold them up. Do you think he had his bottom removed for medical reasons? Or that it got torn off in a terrible accident?"

Observations such as these made the time pass pleasantly. Until they came over the hill and saw in front of them the blue expanse of the ocean stretching out to the horizon.

"Great balls of fire!" exclaimed Nanny Piggins. She often said this when she felt very strongly about something but did not want to say a bad word in front of the children. "We're all going to die!"

"We are?!" said Samantha with genuine concern. She did not want to die in the middle of such a pleasant bus trip.

"Look! The edge of the land has broken off!" cried Nanny Piggins.

Derrick, with a flash of insight, realized Nanny Piggins was talking about the ocean. "It's meant to be that way," he reassured her. Being the eldest, it was his job to pretend to be responsible when adults fell apart.

"But the countryside has fallen away and there's nothing but all that blue stuff," protested Nanny Piggins.

"It's all right. The blue stuff is the ocean," Derrick explained. "That's what you get at the edge of the land. Haven't you ever been to the beach before?"

Nanny Piggins never liked admitting she did not know something. But on this occasion she had to be truthful. "No," she admitted.

"You mean there's actually something you haven't done?" asked Michael in amazement. It seemed to him that his nanny was an expert at everything. She certainly knew a million times more than their father or any of the teachers at their school.

"Didn't your circus ever travel to the beach?" asked Samantha.

"No," said Nanny Piggins sadly. "You see, the Ringmaster had a morbid fear of octopuses, so we always avoided the beach and aquariums."

The children nodded. They could see how a man would be afraid of octopuses.

"I've read about beaches in books, of course," Nanny Piggins told them. "So I know that beaches have sand. But I didn't realize a beach had an ocean as well."

"They all do," said Michael.

"And I didn't realize that an ocean would be quite so big," said Nanny Piggins as she pressed her snout to the glass to get a closer look. "Why, it's bigger than the cake factory in Slimbridge." The Slimbridge cake factory was, to Nanny Piggins, the finest achievement in architecture ever in the world.

Nanny Piggins and the children stared in wonder at the ocean as the bus wound closer toward it.

"I guess that explains why whales are so big," mused Nanny Piggins. "If you live in something as huge as the ocean, you wouldn't notice that you were big yourself. A whale would never have to worry about bumping his head on doorframes or finding trousers that fit."

On arrival at the beach Nanny Piggins's enthusiasm for what she found there was divided. She was enormously in favor of French fries with extra salt and vinegar but she was not entirely convinced about the charms of sand.

She opened up one of the suitcases and sat in the lid of it, eating ice cream as the children built sand castles. She could see the attraction of a sand castle because you could run along the beach and jump on it. Destruction was always invigorating, but she could not forgive sand for its uncomfortable ability to find its way into any clothes and rub unpleasantly.

Then there was the water. Nanny Piggins was not a pig who scared easily, but she was cautious in her approach to the ocean itself. It was so huge compared to her, for she was a petite little pig.

Fortunately, food always made Nanny Piggins feel brave. After some French fries, ice cream, and four or five large cakes, she was feeling courageous, so she and the children ventured toward the water. When the children started to wade in, she became alarmed. "What are you doing?"

"Going for a swim," explained Derrick.

"But what if you get eaten by a shark or a sea monster?" asked Nanny Piggins with genuine concern.

"Don't worry," said Michael reassuringly as he took hold of Nanny Piggins's hand. "Getting eaten by sharks and sea monsters is not nearly as common in real life as it is in books."

So Nanny Piggins joined the children in going for a swim. And it was very pleasant. It was much more exciting than swimming in a pool because there were waves to knock you over if you were not paying attention. And unlike the public swimming pool, you could shriek and scream as loud as you liked because the sound was drowned out by the sea. Admittedly, the water did taste disgusting when Nanny Piggins tried drinking it. As a general rule Nanny Piggins tried eating and drinking most substances just on the off chance that they were delicious. She thought it was very misleading that it was called "water" when it tasted nothing like water from a tap. It was like calling sewage "ginger ale" just because they were both brown.

After the swim, they all toweled off and sat on the beach while Nanny Piggins came up with an idea for what to do next. The children expected her to suggest more sand castles, or a game of soccer, or perhaps digging an enormous hole. That is what most normal people choose to do at the beach. But Nanny Piggins was not normal. A small sailboat caught her eye as it tacked its way across the bay.

"Since we've traveled all this way to get to the seaside," mused Nanny Piggins, "it would be very nice to go beyond the 'side' and actually travel across the sea."

The children looked at each other with mild concern.

"I wonder where we could get a boat?" said Nanny Piggins. "Do you think we would have to commandeer one like pirates?"

"We could," said Samantha, for she did not want to be discouraging. "Or we could rent one." Doing illegal things always worried Samantha, so she was usually the first to suggest a non-illegal alternative. "There's a boat rental place over there on the pier."

"What a brilliant idea!" said Nanny Piggins, because she was not an ungenerous pig and having so many brilliant ideas herself, she was always the first to recognize brilliance in others.

Nanny Piggins struck a happy deal with the boat rental man. In exchange for Mr. Green's favorite wristwatch (which she just happened to have in her pocket), the rental man gave Nanny Piggins and the children his smallest sailing boat and a five-minute lesson on the principles of yachting. And so, despite having almost no idea what they were doing, they sailed off.

Nanny Piggins took to sailing instantly. Having lived her whole life in the circus, she was used to handling ropes and large sheets of canvas. In no time at all, she was happily guiding the boat across the water at a good speed.

The children were enchanted by the experience. The movement of the boat did make Derrick feel violently ill. But apart from that, they enjoyed the sense of freedom. It was like driving a car except better because there were no roads you had to follow. And it was amazing to stare down into the blue depths and think how there was nothing beneath them except water, fish, and possibly the secret city of Atlantis.

"Where shall we go?" asked Nanny Piggins.

"Go?" questioned Derrick. It had not occurred to the children they had the option of going somewhere. They had assumed they would have to go out and come back to where they started. Like on pony rides, go-karts, or any other children's amusement.

"All the seas and all the oceans in the entire world are connected together," said Nanny Piggins, because she did know the important things about geography. "So if we're here on the ocean, that means as long as we point the boat in the right direction we can go anywhere in the world."

"Anywhere in the whole wide world?" gasped Michael. His mouth hung open as his mind overflowed with all the possibilities.

"Anywhere that has an ocean or a sea joining on to it," confirmed Nanny Piggins, "which is just about everywhere, except Luxembourg and Paraguay. We can go there another day."

The children were too stunned to respond. There were so many options. Samantha had always liked penguins and would have loved to visit Antarctica. Derrick liked big stones and would have been fascinated by the giant heads of Easter Island. And Michael liked riding up and down in elevators so he would have loved the tall buildings of New York. But as they sat in the tiny boat, these things did not occur to them. Or rather they occurred to them along with a thousand other ideas all at once so it was impossible for them to pick out just one idea of what to do. Luckily, at this point, Nanny Piggins had another brilliant idea. The third one of the day—which just shows what a good day it was! "I've got it! Let's sail to China!" declared Nanny Piggins. The children all thought this was a wonderful idea for a variety of reasons.

"So we can see the Great Wall of China?" asked Derrick.

"And visit the Chinese entombed warriors?" asked Samantha.

"And learn how to do kung fu?" asked Michael.

"Oh yes, we'll definitely do all that," agreed Nanny Piggins. "But first of all, I want to go because I'm really hungry and I just love Chinese food." So it was agreed that they would set sail for China immediately. Nanny Piggins was not entirely sure which direction China was in but she knew the world was round, and China was very big, so she was confident that if they headed straight out to sea, they would bump into it eventually.

★ ★ ★

It was a windy day and they made quick progress. Within a few short hours they were a long way out to sea. The town they had set sail from shrank down to a tiny dot, then disappeared entirely behind them.

The children were not bored because Nanny Piggins had packed loads of novels and packets of cookies into the suitcases. She had even packed fancy dress costumes. They had great fun for an hour or two dressing up as pirates and pretending to plunder imaginary ships. So even though it was getting to be late afternoon, they were not at all bored or dispirited. They were all looking forward to finding out if the Chinese food in China was even better than the Chinese food everywhere else.

Unfortunately, at this point in the adventure, trouble began to arise. Mainly in the form of a big nasty storm. Huge black clouds gathered in the sky behind them. And a dark gray curtain seemed to hang from the dense cloud mass. It was only when the clouds moved overhead that they realized the gray curtain was in fact very, very heavy rain.

Now Nanny Piggins and the children enjoyed rain as much as anybody who owns a pair of gumboots and knows how to jump in a puddle. But there is rain and then there is *rain*. And *rain* in the quantity they were experiencing was most definitely overwhelming. They had to use their sand buckets to bail rainwater out of the boat. And while they did this, no one was attending to the sail, so the storm winds pushed them farther and farther out into the rough sea.

Obviously Nanny Piggins did not panic. She knew that when you are caught in a very small sailing boat in a very big storm, the worst that can happen is you are shipwrecked, and being shipwrecked is not so bad. All you have to do is spend years and years living on a deserted island until you are eventually rescued by a passing ship. Then you return to civilization and make a fortune writing a fictionalized account of your adventure, which to Nanny Piggins's mind sounded like a pleasant way to spend a decade.

The problem was, until they *were* shipwrecked, sitting in a tiny boat in a downpour was very unpleasant. Nanny Piggins had packed wet-weather gear into the suitcases, so they were all wearing raincoats. Samantha was even wearing Mrs. Green's fishing waders. But there is something about rain: When you get enough of it, it will always find its way in. They were just beginning to feel really cold and miserable and sorry for themselves, when through the rainy gloom, they saw the shape of a boat. Unlike their small sailing boat, this boat was engine-powered, and it chugged through the rain toward them.

"Who do you think it is?" asked Derrick.

"It could be pirates!" said Michael.

"It's best not to get our hopes up," instructed Nanny Piggins. She had always wanted to meet a pirate and being captured by one would be the most exciting way to make their acquaintance.

"If they are wicked, perhaps we should try and avoid them," suggested Samantha. She did not mind being captured herself because she had great faith in her nanny's ability to rescue her, but she was worried about the pirates stealing her boo-boo, a security blanket hidden in the bottom left-hand corner of the blue suitcase, which was, to her, the greatest treasure in the world.

"I don't mind them capturing us," said Nanny Piggins generously. "As long as they drop us off in China before dinnertime. I'm getting hungry."

As it turned out they had little choice in the matter. The wind was so powerful that, even though they had taken down all the sails, they were pushed straight into the side of the larger boat. It made a loud thud and left a nasty gash in the paintwork of both vessels, much to Samantha's concern.

"I hope they don't get cross," said Samantha. She never liked it when people got cross.

"Perhaps we could board them and take them all prisoner," suggested Michael, having had a sudden rush of blood to the head.

"Don't be silly," reprimanded Nanny Piggins. "They might be wicked pirates, but we don't want them to think we're rude."

At that moment two heads appeared over the side of the boat.

"Oh my goodness! Are we in Chinese waters?!" gasped Samantha, because the two men looking down at them were certainly of Asian appearance.

"Don't be silly. Of course we're not," said Nanny Piggins. "Those men are Korean."

To be fair to Samantha, it is hard to guess anyone's nationality in a downpour, at twilight, on the open ocean. And Nanny Piggins did have a clue to help her correct recognition. She had noticed the Korean flag painted on the side of the ship.

"*Ahnyong*," Nanny Piggins called up to the two men. (This is how you say "hello" in Korean.) Nanny Piggins may never have been to the seaside but she had spent many long nights playing backgammon with two Korean trapeze artists. And they had taught her enough Korean to buy a chicken, rent a motorbike, tell someone to be quiet in the cinema, and all the other things essential for day-to-day life.

"*Ahnyong*," the two men called back. They were no doubt surprised to find three children and a Korean-speaking pig adrift in the ocean. But they were hospitable seamen. They soon had Nanny Piggins, Derrick, Samantha, and Michael safely aboard their ship. They also rescued the suitcases, so boo-boo was safe too, much to Samantha's relief.

The Korean ship was a fishing boat with a crew of five men. They were on their way back to port when they had been caught in the storm. But their boat was much better equipped to cope with the turbulent weather than the tiny rental boat. The Koreans had a warm cabin below-decks, a cupboard full of dry towels, and most important of all, a kitchen from which the most delicious smells were emerging.

That night Nanny Piggins and the children learned a valuable lesson: Korean food is every bit as good as Chinese food. Together, Nanny Piggins, the children, and the

"*Ahnyong,*" Nanny Piggins called up to the two men. (This is how you say "hello" in Korean.)

fishermen had a wonderful feast. They ate fresh barbecued fish with steamed vegetables and all sorts of wonderful and peculiar Korean pickles. Then afterward, for dessert, Nanny Piggins opened up the suitcases and found another three chocolate cakes. It was a wonderful party. They played Pin the Tail on the *Tangnagui* (which means "donkey" in Korean) and Go Fish (the fishermen were very good at that game) and generally had a marvelous time.

So they were all quite sad when the fishing boat pulled into the harbor and dropped Nanny Piggins and the children off by the taxi stand. Nanny Piggins tried to persuade the fishermen to come back to Mr. Green's house for a late supper and dancing, but they were tired from a long day of fishing and rescuing small children, so they promised to come another time.

As they sat in the warm taxi winding their way home, Nanny Piggins sighed with contentment. "Well, children, I must say, I never knew that a day at the beach could be so much fun," she said. "We really must do this more often."

"Not too often," said Samantha.

"No, just often enough," said Nanny Piggins.

After a few yawns and some valiant attempts to keep their eyes open, the three children curled up alongside their nanny and they all fell asleep. And in her dreams, Nanny Piggins started to come up with even more brilliant ideas for their next day trip.

CHAPTER SEVEN

Nanny Piggins and the Home Intruder

It was two o'clock in the morning and the house was completely dark. That is not to say that everyone was in bed. Quite the contrary. Mr. Green was away on business, so naturally Nanny Piggins and the children had decided to stay up half the night playing Murder in the Dark. Which is why all the lights were turned off. Usually, when they were all asleep, Mr. Green insisted that lights be left on. This, supposedly, was to fool dim-witted burglars into believing that someone in the house suffered from terrible insomnia and was awake all night every night.

The rules of Murder in the Dark require one person to be elected the murderer. Then everyone creeps around in the darkness until the murderer finds someone and kills them by simply tapping them on the shoulder and whispering "I'm murdering you" in their ear. It is actually a much less violent game than the name suggests. Certainly less violent than most of the games Nanny Piggins and the children liked to play. A lot of injuries did occur but that was not from the murdering. That was from bumping into the furniture while the lights were out.

The current round of Murder in the Dark that Nanny Piggins and the children were playing had been going on for some time—about forty minutes. It is not that they were particularly good at the game. They had simply forgotten to elect a murderer before they started, an easy mistake to make when you are excited to start a new round and it's two o'clock in the morning. Nevertheless, they were all enormously enjoying sneaking around the pitch-black house not getting murdered. The silence was occasionally punctuated by someone crying out "ow" when they bumped into something, or "oops" when they knocked something over.

Finally, at about the forty-minute mark, it did occur

to Nanny Piggins that she could not remember drawing cards to see who would be the murderer before they started the game. And when all was said and done, she was the nanny, which meant she had the leadership role. Much as she naturally disliked doing anything selfless, she took it upon herself to become the murderer. So instead of sneaking around the house from one hiding spot to another, she started to sneak around the house looking for one of the children so she could scare the living daylights out of them.

The problem was that the children were very good at this game. They played it whenever Mr. Green went away, or if he had eaten turkey for dinner and fallen into a really deep sleep. They had also been playing for forty minutes straight. So Derrick, Samantha, and Michael were all very good at avoiding being murdered. Nanny Piggins considered this to be one of the most important life skills. The only downside was the children were very difficult to find when Nanny Piggins wanted to murder them herself.

She crept around the house listening for breathing, chocolate eating, breaking porcelain, or any of the other peculiar little noises children make. But the children must have been breathing exceptionally quietly that night because Nanny Piggins could hear nothing above the tick of the clock and the whirr of the VCR[2] (which had been set to record a horror film, in case the children got tired and thought they wanted to go to bed. It was the type of film that was guaranteed to make them incapable of sleep for days).

This is when the jiggling started. At first it was very quiet and tentative, but then the jiggling became louder and continuous. One of the children was being noisy. Nanny Piggins could not imagine what they were doing. Perhaps disassembling the toaster or trying to slide coins out of a money box with a knife. Nanny Piggins kept moving toward the noise. It was coming from somewhere near the front door. Nanny Piggins crept closer, staying near the wall because the floorboards were less likely to creak there. (It is important in Murder in the Dark that your victim does not know you are coming.

---

[2] The Greens still used a VCR because Mr. Green was too cheap to pay for a DVD recorder or TiVo. In fact they only got the VCR because Mr. Green saw it sticking out of a neighbor's rubbish bin. Then in the middle of the night he crept out and took it, which was the most daring thing he had done in years.

That way they scream a lot louder and it impresses the other players.)

As she got near the front door, the jiggling gave one last final jiggle then stopped. Nanny Piggins stopped too and listened to hear what her victim would do next. She heard the doorknob turn and the door open. None of the children had ever dared go outside before in a game of Murder in the Dark. She had to give them bonus points for initiative. But, in this instance, because she was the murderer, she was not about to let them get away with it. Nanny Piggins hurled herself forward, leaping high into the air in the general direction of the doorway. She met with instant success. Nanny Piggins soon found herself slamming into someone's chest, head, and shoulders, then falling with him to the floor.

"You're murdered!" she whispered conspiratorially in her victim's ear.

"Aaaaaagh!!" screamed her victim, just as a good victim should when playing Murder in the Dark.

Nanny Piggins immediately sprang back to pretend that the murderer was not necessarily her, although she was not able to hide the smug grin on her face after successfully cutting off her victim in the open doorway.

The lights flicked on throughout the house as Derrick, Samantha, and Michael emerged from their various hiding places in different rooms and raced toward the direction of the scream.

Then they all screamed, Nanny Piggins included, when they realized it was not one of them lying dazed on the floor, but a fully grown hoodlum wearing a black ski mask as though he were a burglar.

Fortunately Nanny Piggins quickly recovered from her screaming and had the presence of mind to hit the hoodlum over the head with an umbrella (which is why it is so very important to have an umbrella stand right by the front door). She then tied him up with a roll of string she happened to have in her pocket. Nanny Piggins had been the hog-tying champion of her circus seven years in a row (if you are a pig, it is best to compete in the hog-tying competition just so that nobody gets funny ideas about competing on you). She had the hoodlum trussed up in under twelve seconds. Michael timed her with his watch.

They dragged the hoodlum into the living room and tied him to a chair. Nanny Piggins rather enjoyed tying knots once she got started. Then they all stood back and had a good look at him.

"Do you think he's a murderer?" asked Michael. "You know, a real one."

"Or a kidnapper?" asked Derrick.

"Or a..." Samantha struggled to think of something more exotic than a kidnapper or a murderer. "...a kidnapping murderer who steals jewels?"

"I don't know. It's hard to tell from just looking at him. That's the thing about these criminals. They're very good at disguising themselves," said Nanny Piggins.

"Oi! I'm not a kidnapping murderer," said the hoodlum suddenly.

Nanny Piggins and the children leaped back in surprise.

"My goodness, he speaks English!" exclaimed Nanny Piggins.

"'Course I do," said the hoodlum as he wiggled about, trying to escape the tightly knotted string.

"There's no ''course' about it. If you were an assassin hired by a foreign government to kidnap Mr. Green in his sleep, who knows what language you might speak," said Nanny Piggins.

"Why would anyone want to kidnap Father in his sleep?" asked Samantha. She was not necessarily against the idea but she was curious if Nanny Piggins knew something she did not.

"To get to me, of course," said Nanny Piggins. "To try to force me to give up my sticky date pudding recipe. You'd be amazed at the desperate lengths people will go to for my baking secrets. Once a home economics teacher chained herself to my cannon for a week. She didn't get my recipe but she learned a lot about ballistics."

"I haven't been hired by any foreigners and I've never met the bloke that lives here, I swear," protested the hoodlum.

"You're not allowed to swear in this house," said Michael. "You'll get one less piece of chocolate at dinnertime if you do."

"It's all right, Michael," said Nanny Piggins. "There are two types of swearing and one of them is okay."

"Really?" asked Michael.

"Yes, really," Nanny Piggins assured him. "It's just another confusing thing about the English language, invented to baffle us all."

"Why don't we pull off his ski mask?" suggested Derrick.

"He might bite," warned Nanny Piggins. "I know I

would if I were wearing a ski mask and someone started tugging at it."

"It's all right, I won't bite. I'd like it if you took it off because I'm getting a bit hot," the hoodlum assured them.

"That'll serve you right for breaking into homes while wearing winter clothes in the height of summer," said Nanny Piggins unsympathetically.

Nevertheless, Derrick tugged the hoodlum's ski mask off and they were all disappointed to discover that their hoodlum was not very impressive at all. He was about seventeen years old, skinny, and he had pimples. To Nanny Piggins's mind a kidnapper should at least grow a mustache. That way they have something to twirl when they are laughing evilly over their wicked deeds.

"Just our luck," bemoaned Nanny Piggins. "We're not even attacked by a proper scary hoodlum. We're attacked by a juvenile pimply one."

"I'm not a juvenile," the hoodlum protested. "I turn eighteen next month."

"Mozart was the toast of Europe by the time he was eighteen. Something tells me you're not going to be," said Nanny Piggins.

The children all stared at the hoodlum. They were

almost disappointed that their game of Murder in the Dark had been interrupted by someone so unimpressive.

"If you weren't going to kidnap or murder anybody, what are you doing here?" asked Nanny Piggins.

"I've been watching this house for months. This was the first time all the lights were off. I thought there was nobody home or that the insomniac was cured. So I picked the lock and I was just going to take a few things," admitted the hoodlum.

The children all gasped in horror.

"But stealing is wrong," said Michael. He was deeply shocked.

"I wasn't going to steal much. You rich people always have insurance. So I was just going to take a couple of valuable things," explained the hoodlum.

"Like my bicycle?" asked a shocked Samantha.

"Or my baseball bat?" asked a shocked Derrick.

"Or my ant farm?" asked a shocked Michael.

"Or my collection of romance novels?" asked a shocked Nanny Piggins.

"Nothing like that. I was just after cash or jewelry," said the hoodlum.

"Is that all?! You should have just knocked on the front

door and asked," said Nanny Piggins, rolling her eyes. "We could have told you we don't have any of that here."

"You've got to. Every house has them," argued the hoodlum.

"Not this house. Father doesn't approve of spending money or leaving money anywhere other than in a high-interest savings account," explained Samantha. She had heard her father go on about this many, many times.

"Typical. I've never been able to pick them," admitted the hoodlum.

"Pick what?" asked Derrick.

"Which house to rob by looking at the front garden," said the hoodlum.

"You mean you've done this before!" exclaimed Nanny Piggins. Now she was really shocked.

"Maybe," admitted the hoodlum cautiously.

"But you're so rotten at it, I assumed it was your first time," declared Nanny Piggins.

"I'm not that bad. I got in all right, didn't I? Not just anybody can pick a lock," he protested.

"Yes, but someone with a good deal more sense would have walked around to the back door and found that it was wide open," said Nanny Piggins.

"I didn't think of that," admitted the hoodlum and, for the first time, he actually did look ashamed.

"So what are we going to do with him?" asked Derrick. This was an interesting question. It had not occurred to Nanny Piggins that she would get to "do something" with her newfound hoodlum.

"I suppose we should hand him over to the police," said Samantha. That was certainly what girl detectives always did in all the novels she had read. And Samantha would have quite liked to be a girl detective if it weren't for all the violence and creeping into caves in the middle of the night.

"Hand him over to the police?" asked Nanny Piggins, aghast at such a ridiculous suggestion. "Why on earth would we do that?"

"That is what you're meant to do when you catch a criminal," explained Derrick, "so the authorities can punish him properly."

"But that's just not fair!" protested Nanny Piggins. "We caught him. We should get to do the punishment. Why should we let the proper authorities have all the fun?"

The children could see that Nanny Piggins had a very good point. And since she was meant to be the responsible

They were already looking forward to
seeing what sort of punishment Nanny
Piggins had in mind.

adult pig, and she was paid to be in charge, they were not about to argue with her. They were already looking forward to seeing what sort of punishment Nanny Piggins had in mind.

"You aren't going to beat me, are you?" asked the hoodlum, sounding genuinely worried. "I know my rights," he protested, the way people always do when they know their rights are about to be violated.

"Don't worry, we're not going to beat you," Nanny Piggins assured him with a wistful look on her face. Her mind was already churning over the possibilities. And it turned out that Nanny Piggins had a wonderfully imaginative idea of what punishment should involve.

.... ★ ★ ★ ....

The first punishment Nanny Piggins came up with was forcing the hoodlum to go into the kitchen and bake a double-chocolate-chip chocolate mud cake with chocolate icing and chocolate sauce in the middle. To really teach him a lesson she made him make it from scratch, using actual flour and eggs, not a packet mix from the supermarket.

The hoodlum found this very arduous and difficult. It involved doing one of the things he personally enjoyed least in the world—reading. He had to read all the amounts from the recipe book and measure them out exactly, which he complained was just like being back at school and studying math again. But Nanny Piggins had no mercy. She watched him like a hawk, making sure he followed the recipe to the letter. If you are going to eat a double-chocolate-chip chocolate mud cake with chocolate icing, it might as well be a really good double-chocolate-chip chocolate mud cake with chocolate icing.

By the time he had finished, the poor hoodlum was covered in flour and drenched in sweat. Beating butter into sugar is not as easy as it looks. It takes a surprising amount of upper-body strength. But Nanny Piggins was not prepared to let him rest on his laurels. She had more punishments in mind.

Next she got him to sand back the wall in the hallway bathroom and repaint the whole room entirely. She had been meaning to do this herself for weeks, ever since she accidentally set fire to the paintwork when she was having a candlelit bath. It had been a pain persuading Mr. Green to go to work every morning without going to the toilet.

The hoodlum had never done any painting before and it seemed he was not very gifted at it. He kept bumping into things, and tripping over things, and flicking specks of paint into his own eyes at crucial moments. By the time he was done, the walls were not the only thing covered in periwinkle blue paint—he was as well.

"Can I stop now, please?" he begged. "My arms hurt, I've banged my shin, and I've got a headache from the paint fumes."

"Of course you can stop painting," said Nanny Piggins. "As soon as you've finished the second coat."

The hoodlum looked as if he was going to cry as he trudged back into the bathroom. The punishment did not stop there. When she had time to think about it, Nanny Piggins came up with all sorts of interesting chores for him. She made him chop wood. And not just from big logs into smaller logs. She made him climb over into Mrs. McGill's garden and cut down her tree (it had been dead for ten years and was a terrible safety hazard. But Mrs. McGill was too mean to do anything about it. She secretly liked it when branches fell off and hit pedestrians on the head).

Nanny Piggins also made the hoodlum retile the roof,

catch every cockroach in the basement, prune Mr. Green's rose bushes, rewire all the lights, learn to dance the tango, mow the lawn, unblock the kitchen sink, hand sew five thousand sequins onto an evening dress, and vacuum the house.

Then Nanny Piggins made the hoodlum do the most awful job of all. She made him do all the children's French homework. He begged to be allowed to go back to hand-washing Mr. Green's smelly socks but Nanny Piggins was very strict with him. He wasn't going anywhere until he had conjugated all the verbs.

And so, as the sun started to peek above the horizon in the early hours of the morning, the house was beautifully clean and painted, the children's homework was done, and they all sat around the kitchen table eating chocolate mud cake. Everyone, especially the hoodlum, agreed that he had been thoroughly punished.

"You certainly know how to put a young man off a life of crime, Nanny Piggins. I'm going to have dishpan hands for a month," said the hoodlum as he sadly looked at his chafed and blistered fingers.

"I hope you've learned your lesson. You should never ever break into a house and steal things. Because you never know when you might be attacked by a flying pig," said Nanny Piggins.

"You've got that right. I've learned my lesson," the hoodlum assured her. "I'm going straight now."

"Straight where?" asked Michael.

"I mean, I've gone off a life of crime and I'm going to get a proper job," explained the hoodlum.

"Doing what?" asked Samantha, not believing that anyone in their right mind would actually pay the hoodlum to come into an office wearing a suit and tie and do paperwork like her father.

"Well, look at all the things I've learned how to do tonight," said the hoodlum. "I've learned how to chop wood, paint a wall, catch cockroaches, unblock drains, rewire electric lights, sew a dress, and bake a chocolate cake. I reckon I'm fully trained up to be an odd-jobs man."

"What a good idea!" exclaimed Nanny Piggins. "And you already knew how to pick locks. So you will be able to let people into their homes when they've locked themselves out as well."

"Yeah, I'll need a van, of course, but I can always nick one and..." the hoodlum began.

"A-a-ah," remonstrated Nanny Piggins, glaring at him.

"I could always borrow one and return it to its owner when I have saved the money to buy my own."

"That's better," said Nanny Piggins.

"I'd best be off, or my mom will be wondering where I've gotten to," said the hoodlum.

"But who says your punishment is over?" asked Nanny Piggins imperiously.

"Oh come on, it is, isn't it?" begged the hoodlum. "I don't reckon I could do any more. I think I've strained my innards."

"I guess if your innards are strained then you've probably learned your lesson," conceded Nanny Piggins.

So Nanny Piggins and the children said good-bye to their hoodlum. Then they all went to bed fully content with their wonderful night of murder and punishment.

CHAPTER EIGHT

Nanny Piggins and the Fugitive

anny Piggins and the children were sitting in the living room playing poker when they were interrupted by a loud knock at the front door. At first, Nanny Piggins pretended she had not heard it. She had two aces and did not want to lose her opportunity to win the jelly beans they were playing for. But then the knock sounded again and this time it was even louder.

"I think there's someone at the door," said Derrick. He did not look up from his cards either, and he certainly did not volunteer to answer it. He had three jacks and he knew his nanny well enough to know she would alter his cards while he was out of the room, to teach him a lesson about not leaving your cards in the middle of a game.

The knock came again. Whoever was there was clearly not going away.

Nanny Piggins sighed. "Someone has to answer the door," she said. "Is anybody going to volunteer?"

"Father told us to never open the door to strangers," said Samantha. Which was, in fact, true. But she knew she was using the truth conveniently because she had a full house (a three of a kind and a pair), which was a very good hand, and she particularly liked eating jelly beans.

"Let's decide this democratically," suggested Nanny Piggins. "Hands up — who thinks Michael should answer the door?"

Samantha's and Derrick's hands shot up immediately. Michael gasped at how cleverly he had been outwitted.

"Run along, Michael, you've been democratically elected to open the front door so you better get on with it," said Nanny Piggins.

Michael left the room grumbling about "unfairness"

and "mean older people." He was just reaching for the front door when the knock came again. "I'm coming, I'm coming, keep your hair on," said Michael discourteously. But as he swung open the door all thoughts of etiquette flew out of his head. He stood agape for one split second before slamming the door shut and running screaming back to Nanny Piggins.

"Aaaaaaaaaaaaaaaaaggggggggggghhhhhh!!!!" said Michael, bursting into the kitchen just as Nanny Piggins was scraping all the jelly beans into her pocket because she had won the hand.

"What is it? What's wrong?" Nanny Piggins asked.

The running and the screaming had, however, left Michael temporarily unable to answer. Instead he gasped for breath and pointed meaningfully at the front door.

"He's probably just been stung by a bee," said Derrick. His mind was still on the jelly beans.

"If he has been stung by a bee, that is very serious indeed," said Nanny Piggins. She did not approve of older brothers being callous when their younger brothers were in pain. "Bees are very silly creatures. They always overreact terribly. Ladybugs get along just fine without stinging people. I don't see why bees have to be so violent." This was an issue Nanny Piggins felt quite strongly about, having been stung by several dozen bees once, while trying to suck the honey out of a beehive. The honey was delicious but, on the whole, not worth the pain and swelling.

"It wasn't a bee," gasped Michael. "It was a bear!"

"I didn't know bears could sting," said Samantha. She was not concentrating either. She was still not entirely sure that Nanny Piggins's pair should have beaten her full house.

"It didn't sting me. I slammed the door on it as quick as I could before it could attack," protested Michael.

"A bear, you say?" said Nanny Piggins. Michael now had her full attention.

"It'll just be one of Michael's crazy stories again. He's probably been staying up all night reading picture books with a flashlight. It always sends him loopy," said Derrick as he inspected his brother for dark rings under the eyes or other telltale signs of excessive nighttime reading.

"There is nothing wrong with reading picture books all night. A young man should stay informed," said Nanny

Piggins, defending Michael. "But tell me about this bear. What did he look like?"

"He was a big one," said Michael, pleased at last that someone was taking him seriously.

"Was his fur brown?" asked Nanny Piggins.

"Yes," said Michael.

"Were his teeth yellow?" asked Nanny Piggins.

"Yes," said Michael.

"And were his eyes the same color blue as a Swiss lake on a hot summer's day?" asked Nanny Piggins.

"Why yes, they were," said Michael, suddenly remembering that the vicious bear did have remarkably pretty eyes.

Nanny Piggins abruptly stood up. "I thought as much," she declared. Then, abandoning the card game on the floor, she bravely marched to the front door herself.

"Shouldn't you call the police?" called Derrick.

"Or the Royal Society for the Prevention of Cruelty to Animals," suggested Samantha.

"Or the Royal Society for Plenty of Cruelty to Animals," suggested Michael, thinking that, if it was a vicious bear, cruelty might be more appropriate. None of the Green children wanted to see Nanny Piggins torn limb from limb by a wild animal in front of their very eyes. She was by far the best nanny they had ever had. She let them keep ferrets in their bedrooms, drive their father's ride-on lawn mower to the store, and eat nothing but sweets for dinner, all the time.

Nevertheless, without hesitating or even turning around to say good-bye, Nanny Piggins threw open the front door and confronted the giant hulking bear still standing on the doorstep. But instead of screaming and being torn into tiny pieces, Nanny Piggins opened her arms wide and cried out, "Boris!"

"Sarah!" replied the bear.

And they fell into each other's arms, sharing an enormous bear hug, which is the only type of hug bears do.

"Crikey," said Michael. "I think they know each other."

And indeed they did. Nanny Piggins soon brought Boris into the house and explained all about him. "Children," she announced, "this is my brother, Boris the dancing bear."

Boris did a pirouette to demonstrate how he came by the title. Then they all sat down to eat jelly beans and become firm friends.

"How can a pig have a bear as a brother?" asked Derrick.

"Children," she announced, "this is my brother, Boris the dancing bear."

He did not want to appear rude but he was burning with curiosity. And Nanny Piggins always had enthralling explanations for all the most peculiar things.

"Boris is my adopted brother," she explained.

"But I didn't know you had parents," quizzed Samantha.

"You don't have to have parents to have a brother. In fact, it is a lot easier if you don't," explained Nanny Piggins. "Boris has been my brother ever since he arrived at the circus in a crate sent from Russia."

"Why Russia?" asked Derrick.

"What do these children learn in school?" asked Boris, horrified by their ignorance.

"Not much," Nanny Piggins admitted. "I have to teach them all the important things myself." And turning to the children she explained this too. "All the best ballet dancers come from Russia. So when the circus decided they wanted a dancing bear, they wrote to the Russian Ballet. And it just so happened that Boris was their star. They don't usually let bears join, of course. But he was so good at dancing on his tippy toes, they didn't even realize he was a bear until he'd been there three weeks, by which time they'd all been enchanted by his flying leaps."

"It's true," said Boris, with a complete lack of modesty.

"When Boris arrived at the circus I was just a piglet and he was only eight feet tall. Of course we hit it off immediately when we discovered we had a shared love of honey in all its forms: honeycomb, honey mustard dressing, honey straight out of the jar.... So we adopted each other as brother and sister," explained Nanny Piggins.

"Being a lonely orphan is fun, but it is even more fun when you can share it with a sister," said Boris.

"Obviously it was difficult when Boris first arrived, because he didn't speak a word of English and I didn't speak Russian. So for the first six months we communicated solely through dance."

"How did that work?" asked Michael.

"Well, if I wanted a cup of tea, I would do this." Nanny Piggins got up and gracefully threw herself into a perfect little dance depicting a thirsty pig gasping for refreshment until her thoughtful brother brought her a warm drink. The children clapped. She really was very good.

"And if I wanted to borrow Sarah's hand cream, I would do this." Boris got up and elegantly began his own miniature ballet depicting a hardworking bear whose paws became sadly chafed by his daily chores until an angelic pig thoughtfully bestowed a tube of cream upon him and all was right with the world again. The children applauded again. He was seriously good too.

"So, what are you doing here?" Nanny Piggins asked Boris. "Surely you're the star of the circus now that I've left and they don't have a flying pig anymore."

"Oh, Sarah, you can't imagine how things have changed since you went away. The crowds don't want to see the ballet anymore. They want to see…" Boris paused as he struggled to control his emotions. He could not bring himself to say the words. But eventually after several deep breaths he spat it out. "They want to see… modern dance."

Nanny Piggins gasped. "But you are the finest ballet-dancing bear in all the world," she protested.

"I know, I know, but the Ringmaster, he says that ballet is for… fuddy-duddies." At this point Boris broke down completely and cried loudly into his handkerchief.

"You poor, poor bear," comforted Nanny Piggins. "You must never go back there. They are obviously barbarians who have no appreciation of a great artist."

"*Da*," sobbed Boris. (*Da* is Russian for "yes." Boris always regressed to speaking Russian when he was truly upset.) "But what am I to do? Where am I to go?"

"You can stay here, of course," said Nanny Piggins. "I'm sure the children won't mind."

The children were delighted at the prospect of having an actual giant dancing bear living in their home. Samson Wallace, an acquaintance from school, had been driving them up the wall. All week he had boasted about his new guinea pig. So getting a giant Russian dancing bear would certainly shut him up.

Plus their time with Nanny Piggins had taught them that circus people are much more likely to have interesting things happen to them than regular people. They were sure to have twice as many adventures with two circus stars living in their house. But the children were not naive, so it soon occurred to them that their father would not be quite so open-minded about taking in a ten-foot-tall dancing bear.

Derrick cleared his throat and bravely broached the subject. "The only thing is, Nanny Piggins, I think Father might be a bit difficult about it."

"Of course we can't tell your father," declared Nanny Piggins, surprised that the thought had even occurred to Derrick. She firmly believed in informing Mr. Green about as little as possible. "We'll just have to hide him in the house." Both Boris and Nanny Piggins seemed perfectly content with this plan. But the children saw a potential flaw.

"The only thing is, Nanny Piggins," said Samantha, tentatively because she did not want to appear stupid, "Boris is rather large. Although I'm sure he's very petite for a bear," she quickly added, not wanting to hurt Boris's feelings. "Don't you think it would be quite hard to hide a ten-foot-tall bear from Father?"

Nanny Piggins and Boris just laughed. "Oh my dear, you have so much to learn," said Nanny Piggins. "There are no limits to what a man will fail to notice. Human men are the most unobservant, inattentive creatures in the entire world."

"They're even worse than rhinoceroses," added Boris. "And everyone knows rhinoceroses are very silly."

"How many times have you seen your father looking for his glasses when he was actually wearing them?" asked Nanny Piggins. Samantha had to admit that the answer was quite a few. "And how many times has he searched for his keys when he was holding them in his hand?" added Nanny Piggins. And again Samantha could remember this happening on many occasions.

"Besides, your father leaves for work so early in the morning and returns so late at night," said Nanny Piggins, "I'm sure it will be no trouble at all hiding Boris for a year or two, until he finds a place of his own."

Unfortunately, they never got to find out if this was true. Because the very next day when Nanny Piggins, Boris, and the children were in the middle of playing a rowdy game of tag across the living room, they were interrupted by Mr. Green himself walking in through the front door. Boris, with his quick-thinking Russian intelligence, hastily stuffed a lamp shade on his head and stood very still in the corner, pretending to be a lamp. And Mr. Green was so consumed with his own drama that he did not notice him.

Obviously, Nanny Piggins did not like it when Mr. Green walked into his own house unexpectedly. Under close questioning she soon discovered that he had been sent home from work after collapsing from a stress attack. Apparently he had flown into an apoplectic rage when someone had put sweetener instead of sugar in his coffee, then passed out when he yelled so much that there was not enough oxygen flowing into his brain. A doctor had been called, and ordered him to get bed rest and to take up a relaxing hobby.

For Nanny Piggins and the children, this was their worst nightmare come true. Mr. Green was not a pleasant invalid. He just lay on the couch all day, complaining about every noise and demanding things to be fetched for him. Poor Boris had to go on pretending to be a lamp for six long hours before Mr. Green dozed off and he was able to sneak out of the room.

"What are we going to do? We need to find somewhere to hide Boris before your father finds him and has him shipped back to Russia," said Nanny Piggins.

"I don't want to go back to Russia," sobbed Boris. "It is so cold and they don't have salt-and-vinegar chips there."

The children agreed they could not let Boris go back to such a horrible place. They needed a better hiding spot.

"How about the attic?" suggested Samantha.

"Or the cellar?" suggested Derrick.

"The attic and the cellar are the two places people always hide in storybooks," added Michael.

"I can't go in the cellar. I'm afraid of the dark," confessed Boris.

"The attic it is then," decided Nanny Piggins.

So she and the children spent the next two hours helping Boris climb up the outside of the house and in through the attic window (he couldn't go up the staircase without passing Mr. Green in the living room). It was a noisy operation because Nanny Piggins had to use a chain saw to make the window bigger. But Boris was soon in and safely hidden.

"Right, now we just have to find your father a hobby," said Nanny Piggins.

"Do we really?" asked Derrick. "Couldn't we just leave him alone?" Derrick sometimes went for weeks without speaking to his father and he found he quite liked it that way.

"The doctor said he had to find a relaxing hobby. Besides, the sooner he relaxes the sooner he will go back to work and then the rest of us can relax," reasoned Nanny Piggins.

"But what sort of hobby would Father like?" asked Samantha.

"Good question," said Nanny Piggins as she pondered the problem. "Knowing your father, it has to be a really boring one. He only seems to be interested in boring things."

"How about cooking?" suggested Derrick.

"That's not boring. Besides, if he cooked something he might expect us to eat it. We don't want to risk that," said Nanny Piggins.

"How about jogging?" suggested Samantha.

"That *is* boring. But it would make him healthier. And we don't want that. The last thing we want is for him to have more energy," Nanny Piggins pointed out.

"I've got it! How about stamp collecting?" suggested Michael.

"Stamp collecting? That's not a hobby," protested Nanny Piggins.

"Yes, it is," argued Michael. "I read about it in a book. People used to do it back in the olden days."

"The things people used to do before television. It's heartbreaking," observed Nanny Piggins, shaking her head.

So Nanny Piggins and the children gave Mr. Green a scrapbook and a large pile of stamps, which they had obtained by following the postman as he delivered the mail, then tearing the stamps off the envelopes before the people in the houses came out to collect them. And for the first time in years, Mr. Green was actually delighted with something other than tax law. He took the stamps and the scrapbook up to his bedroom so he could enjoy them in peace.

"That ought to keep him quiet for a few hours. Perhaps Boris will have time to climb down and play handball with us in the garden," mused Nanny Piggins.

But it was not to be. She was just fetching the ladder and the chain saw to get Boris out, when she heard screams coming from Mr. Green's bedroom.

Nanny Piggins and the children rushed up the stairs to see what had happened.

"The ceiling has fallen in!" Mr. Green screamed when they burst in through the door. And there was indeed a large slab of ceiling lying in the middle of his bed, across Mr. Green's lap. As well as dust and dirt everywhere. Mr. Green's new stamp collection had been either ruined by the fallen ceiling, or blown about the room by the impact.

"I heard a scream, then stamping, and then the ceiling fell right on me!" yelled Mr. Green. "Which one of you children was playing in the attic?"

Nanny Piggins was not about to admit there was a bear in the attic, but she did not want the children blamed either, so she hastily concocted a cover story. "I was in the attic," she declared. "I was practicing my line dancing. I didn't think you would mind, because there was nothing in my contract forbidding me from line dancing in the attic when you were home sick from work. But if you tell me now that you would prefer that I didn't, then of course I shall never do it again."

"Of course I don't want you line dancing in the attic," yelled Mr. Green, because he really could be very disagreeable when he put his mind to it.

A short time later Nanny Piggins had calmed Mr. Green down and got him settled in the kitchen, where he was trying his hand at flower arranging. Nanny Piggins had assured him this was a very relaxing hobby, much better than stamp collecting because there was less danger of paper cuts.

Meanwhile, the children had smuggled Boris out of the attic. He explained that the only reason he had stamped a hole through the floor (floor to him but ceiling to Mr. Green) was because he had seen a spider. And that he had always been afraid of spiders and surely Mr. Green should be grateful that someone was trying to exterminate them from the house.

The children decided to hide Boris in the cellar instead. He could stamp as much as he liked down there because the floor was made of earth and could not give way. There was the small matter of Boris's fear of darkness to overcome but the children soon solved that by lending Boris a flashlight.

And so peace was again restored to the household. Mr. Green happily arranged gladiolus in the kitchen, and Boris was safely hidden where he could not possibly be found. Sadly, the peace did not last long. Mr. Green was just adding the final sprig to his display when a hole was suddenly punched up through the floor beneath him. As a result, the table leg fell into the hole and his beautiful arrangement slid off the table, through the hole, and into the cellar.

"What in the blazes is going on?" Mr. Green screamed.

It took all of Nanny Piggins's flattery and a whole pot of chamomile tea to calm him down again. Eventually, Nanny Piggins left Mr. Green lying on the sofa with a wet flannel over his face, and went to find out for herself what had happened.

Boris and the children were sitting on the back step. The children were patting him and feeding him chocolate cookies to calm his nerves.

"What happened?" asked Nanny Piggins.

"The batteries in the flashlight ran out and everything went dark. So Boris panicked and punched a hole up through the floor," explained Samantha.

"I told you I don't like the dark," said Boris sadly. He really did look quite pitiful. If he had not been covered in brown fur, he would have been as white as a sheet.

"There, there, dear. We'll sort something out," Nanny Piggins assured him.

"But what are we going to do?" asked Derrick despairingly. "Who knows how long Father will be at home trying to relax. He doesn't seem to be very good at it, and a ten-foot-tall dancing bear who is afraid of spiders and the dark is a lot harder to hide than you would think."

"True, very true," agreed Nanny Piggins.

The five of them sat and thought very hard for a full five minutes. Michael thought of ice cream. But the rest of them thought of either restful hobbies for Mr. Green or huge, well-lit hiding places for Boris.

"I've got it!" exclaimed Nanny Piggins.

"Got what?" asked Samantha.

"I know how we can kill two birds with one stone," Nanny Piggins declared.

"Oh please, don't kill any birds on my account. I'm a vegetarian," said Boris.

"It's a figure of speech," explained Nanny Piggins. "I mean, I know how to help Mr. Green relax and hide Boris at the same time."

.... ★ ★ ★ ....

Later that afternoon Nanny Piggins, the children, and Boris (as he crouched hidden under a large pile of dirty laundry in the laundry basket) sat on the back doorstep watching Mr. Green. He was really enjoying himself. He had a cordless telephone in one hand and the telephone book in the other. When he was not bossing people around through the phone, he was yelling at three workmen who were busily constructing an enormous garden shed.

"What on earth did you say to Father?" asked Derrick. "You seem to have completely cured him."

"I told him he'd been awarded a luxury garden shed for his services to tax law," said Nanny Piggins simply.

"But Father doesn't like gardening. He hates getting his hands dirty," said Samantha.

"And he doesn't like plants," added Michael.

"And he detests sunshine," added Derrick.

"Yes, but he loves ordering around tradesmen. Look how much fun he's having," said Nanny Piggins, pointing to the construction.

"Where did you get the garden shed?" asked Michael shrewdly.

"Oh, didn't I mention? I won it in a limerick competition at the hardware store," said Nanny Piggins. "I was the only entrant to find one hundred seventeen rhymes for the word *orange*."

"It's huge," observed Samantha.

"I know. Your father will really enjoy boasting all about his shed to everyone at work tomorrow," said Nanny Piggins.

"He's going back to work tomorrow?" asked Michael, completely failing to hide his delight.

"Of course. You can't expect a man to get a shed as impressive as that and not go in to work to boast about it," said Nanny Piggins.

"But he's not actually going to do any gardening, is he?" asked Derrick, slightly concerned that his father might dig up the lawn and destroy their soccer field.

"Goodness no, he won't have time when he goes back to work, will he?" explained Nanny Piggins with a wink.

"Nanny Piggins, you're a genius!" exclaimed Derrick.

"True, very true," murmured Nanny Piggins contently as she sipped on her lemonade.

"But what about me?" whispered Boris.

They had completely forgotten about him. The dirty laundry was such a convincing disguise.

"Well, isn't it obvious?" said Nanny Piggins. "You're going to live in your brand-new home: Mr. Green's shed. It's well lit so you needn't be afraid of the dark. It's brand-new so there won't be any spiders. And after today Mr. Green will never go anywhere near it again. Humans are always getting themselves things like Thighmasters and bread makers, then never using them. They have such poor attention spans."

"My own shed," sobbed Boris. "If my friends in Russia could see me now, they would be so jealous." Boris broke down completely again, but this time he was crying tears of joy. Fortunately Mr. Green was so enjoying bossing the workmen around he did not even notice the shuddering pile of dirty laundry.

CHAPTER NINE

Nanny Piggins and the Ringmaster's Revenge

anny Piggins was spending a pleasant morning helping the children forge sick notes. Technically, there was no need for forgery—Nanny Piggins was the children's nanny so she could legitimately write the notes herself. But Nanny Piggins believed that learning to forge sick notes was an important life skill. As a boring old person once said: "Give a man a fish and he'll eat for a day; teach a man to fish and he'll never go hungry again." Or in this case, teach a child to forge a sick note and he will never have to go to school on cross-country day again. Nanny Piggins was not a great fan of exercise at the best of times. But the idea of forcing children to run great distances across open countryside was, to her mind, a barbaric torture that ought to be made illegal.

Nanny Piggins was just showing Michael how to get exactly the right flourish in the capital G of Mr. Green's signature (she had mastered this herself when they had needed a check to replace the Ming vase broken while playing dodgeball at the City Museum) when someone knocked loudly on the front door. This person had to knock because Nanny Piggins had disconnected the doorbell to discourage the truancy officer. Although, from the loudness of this knock, it was clear they were not going to be so easily deterred.

"Who's that?" asked Boris in a muffled voice. Muffled because he was practicing yoga, so his legs were bent back over his head at the time. Boris was very good at yoga. Being the best ballet-dancing bear in the world, he was very flexible.

"Shhh," whispered Nanny Piggins. "Everyone be quiet while I peek through the curtains and see if it's the truancy officer."

The truancy officer had become well known at the Green house since Nanny Piggins had become their nanny. Nanny Piggins did not often pull the children out of school. But when she did, it was always for blatantly illegitimate reasons. Like the time she burst into Headmaster Pimplestock's office at two o'clock in the afternoon insisting that the children had to come home instantly because their aunt had just died of spontaneous combustion. The headmaster dutifully sent for the children and packed them off with his heartfelt condolences. Then later that day, he saw Michael, Samantha, and Derrick on the television, cheering loudly at the horse races. Ever since then the truancy officer had been a regular visitor.

Nanny Piggins crept along the floor and popped her head up so she could see over the windowsill. (There were lace curtains so she could see out, but outsiders could not see in.) Nanny Piggins could not recognize the visitor immediately because he had his back to her, with his face pressed up against the frosted glass of the front door. From the little she could see, Nanny Piggins could tell it was not the truancy officer. The truancy officer was a freakishly tall woman whereas this appeared to be an unusually short man. Nanny Piggins believed it was beyond the capabilities of the truancy officer to disguise herself so well. But then, as the unusually short man stepped back, Nanny Piggins suddenly recognized him. She recoiled in horror.

"Oh Dear Chocolate! He found me!" she exclaimed.

"What's wrong?" asked Samantha.

"Who is it?" asked Boris.

"Is it a new truancy officer?" asked Michael.

"It's worse than the truancy officer," declared Nanny Piggins.

"How can anybody be worse than the truancy officer?" asked Derrick.

This was the first time the children had ever seen their nanny genuinely frightened. And her being frightened made them feel frightened.

"It's the Ringmaster from the circus!" cried Nanny Piggins.

The children gasped in shock. Boris yelped with fear and hid behind the curtains.

"But how did he find you?" asked Samantha with amazement.

"Who knows? The secret service, phone tapping,

satellite tracking...I wouldn't put anything past him," said Nanny Piggins as she dabbed her forehead with a handkerchief.

The children crawled over to the window to have a peek. They wanted to see this evil genius for themselves. But no sooner had they raised their eyes above the windowsill than they too recoiled in horror. The Ringmaster had his face pressed against the outside of the glass, trying to look in.

"What does he want?" whispered Michael.

"Isn't it obvious? What would any self-respecting Ringmaster want with an internationally famous flying pig?" declared Nanny Piggins.

The children did not know.

"He wants to take me back to the circus to be the star attraction and make lots and lots of money," explained Nanny Piggins.

"The cad," said Derrick

"What are you going to do?" asked Samantha. "You aren't going to let him take you, are you?"

"Of course I'm not going to let him take me," snapped Nanny Piggins. "What kind of pig do you think I am? All we need is an ingenious plan."

"Do you have one?" asked Michael. He loved all of Nanny Piggins's plans, especially ones that involved chocolate.

"You could drop a piano on his head," suggested Boris from behind the curtain.

"Hmm." Nanny Piggins considered this. "That idea does have merit but we don't have a piano. And how would we get him to stand still while we went out, bought a piano, dragged it up the stairs, and shoved it out a window directly above him? No, we'll have to think of something else."

"You'd better think of something quickly," said Derrick as he took another peek out the window, "because he's climbing in through the upstairs bathroom window."

"Typical—you can never trust circus folk," muttered Nanny Piggins.

"But you're circus folk," said Samantha.

"Exactly," said Nanny Piggins. "And how many times have you seen me climb in through Mrs. Simpson's bathroom window when we need to borrow a cup of sugar or her television guide?"

All the children knew this happened quite a lot. Indeed, Mrs. Simpson knew it happened quite a lot. But

Nanny Piggins was always very generous about giving her Mr. Green's first edition books and scaring away Mrs. Simpson's grandchildren when they came to visit, so Mrs. Simpson did not begrudge Nanny Piggins the sugar or the loan of the television guide.

As Nanny Piggins and the children listened they heard a thud, then a toilet flush, then a thump, then the sound of a short man swearing. The Ringmaster had obviously made it into the house.

"Children, you must prepare yourselves," whispered Nanny Piggins. "I am about to engage in a battle of wits with an evil man whose extreme cunning is matched only by my own. You may hear me say some things that are not in the strictest sense true. Your job is to support these fictional accounts to the best of your abilities. Do you understand?"

The children did not really understand but they said yes anyway, because they sensed that the least they could do was be supportive.

They held their breath as they listened to the Ringmaster creep down the stairs. The children did not know what to expect next but they assumed the Ringmaster would yell angrily and threaten them with the Naughty

"Typical—you can never trust circus folk,"
muttered Nanny Piggins.

Step. That is what their father would do, and they assumed all wicked men were much the same. So it came as a complete surprise to them when the door swung open and the Ringmaster burst in with a big smile, saying, "Sarah Piggins! Darling, where have you been? I've been so worried." He then took Nanny Piggins in his arms and kissed her twice on each cheek.

The children looked at Nanny Piggins in openmouthed awe, waiting to see what she would do.

And of course, being Nanny Piggins, she did not disappoint them. She stomped hard on the Ringmaster's foot, saying, "I have never seen you before in my life. I have absolutely no idea what you're talking about."

You had to hand it to Nanny Piggins; she was never cowardly when it came to inventing an alternative to the truth.

"Sarah Piggins, how can you say that when we have worked together for so many happy years?" protested the Ringmaster, still smiling even as he rubbed his crushed toes.

"Sarah Piggins?" said Nanny Piggins. "My name is not Sarah Piggins. My name is Katerina Muellerstock."

"Sarah Piggins, really," said the Ringmaster, wagging

his finger at her as though she was just a naughty little girl and not a fully grown pig with a genius for deceit. "I think I know the world's greatest flying pig when I see her."

"Sarah Piggins…Sarah Piggins…" mused Nanny Piggins. "That name is vaguely familiar. Now where have I heard it before?" She rubbed her snout as she pondered this. "I do have an identical twin sister called Sarah Piggins. And I seem to recall that she decided to pursue a career in flying. That must be it. You must have mistaken me for my twin sister. I'm terribly sorry I stomped on your foot. If I had known you were a friend of my sister's when you broke into our home and burst in upon us, I would merely have given you a wedgie."

"Your twin sister?" said the Ringmaster. "What an amazing story. Of course it is impossible to prove whether or not it is true."

"Not even with DNA testing," said Nanny Piggins, for she had read a lot about genetics. It is important to know what is scientifically possible when you hide your identity.

"But in a way, if I were a callous man," said the Ringmaster with an evil glint in his eye, leaving them all in no doubt that he was a callous man, "it would not matter to me whether you were Sarah Piggins or Sarah Piggins's twin sister. If you are an identical twin then you would have the same weight, size, and shape. So you would be just as good at being fired out of a cannon."

"But you can't force someone to do something they don't want to do!" protested Derrick.

"Oh yes I can!" exclaimed the Ringmaster. "Especially when they have signed an exclusive, binding, fifty-year contact!" With that he whipped a bundle of papers out of his pocket and showed it to the children. It clearly had EXCLUSIVE, BINDING FIFTY-YEAR CONTRACT at the top and Nanny Piggins's distinctive signature at the bottom.

"According to the terms of the contract," said the Ringmaster as he took out his reading glasses and read from the papers, "I am legally entitled to scoop Sarah Piggins up, put her in a sack, and drag her back to the circus whether she wants to come or not."

The children looked at the small print and this was indeed what it said. Circus contracts are notoriously broad.

"How unfortunate for my sister that she did not seek legal advice before signing such a criminally insane contract," said Nanny Piggins. "Indeed, knowing how cunningly ingenious my sister is, I can't help but wonder whether her chocolate cake was drugged to make her sign." Nanny Piggins glared at the Ringmaster meaningfully.

"Sadly it is very hard to prove whether a chocolate cake was drugged years after it was eaten," said the Ringmaster. "The fact is, I need a flying pig. Attendance has been down since she ran away. Even replacing that stupid ballet-dancing bear with flamenco-dancing flamingos didn't draw bigger crowds." (The curtains twitched as he said this because Boris was standing behind them shaking with rage.)

"I am not going to rest until I have a flying pig." With that, the Ringmaster marched to the door. "Good day, Katerina. I shall return this evening at eight pm. Please be packed and ready to leave." Then, with a dramatic flourish, he bowed, spun around, put his hat on, and left. Circus folk know how to leave a room.

"What are we going to do?" wailed Samantha.

"You can't go back to the circus. You just can't," protested Michael.

"I can't believe he didn't want me back as well," sobbed Boris, still behind the curtains.

"I thought you didn't want to go back," said Michael.

"I don't want to go back. But I wanted him to want me to go back," wept Boris. Samantha hugged his leg kindly.

"Do you think he really believed you were your own twin sister?" asked Derrick.

"I don't see why not. Never underestimate the stupidness of a stupid person," said Nanny Piggins.

"I thought you said he was a cunning genius?" said Samantha.

"Even geniuses can be stupid sometimes," said Nanny Piggins. "In fact they are often more stupid than ordinary people. Look at Einstein. He came up with the theory of relativity. But he was too addle-brained to get a haircut."

"The Ringmaster didn't even care if you weren't you. He was threatening to take you anyway," wailed Samantha.

"Yes, I picked up on that. There are no depths circus folk won't sink to," said Nanny Piggins.

"But you're circus folk," pointed out Michael for the second time.

"I know," admitted Nanny Piggins. "And I am ashamed to admit this. But I too have used my circus powers for evil."

"How?" asked Derrick, scandalized, but excited as well.

"I once had myself fired through an open window at the cinema just so I wouldn't have to pay for the ticket," confessed Nanny Piggins.

"Oh gosh!" said Samantha.

"I know. I'm not proud of it," admitted Nanny Piggins. "Although I am proud of my landing. I did a perfect somersault into an empty seat in the middle of the back row. I didn't disturb anyone, unlike those people who actually walk in front of people to get to their seats."

"What are we going to do about the Ringmaster?" asked Derrick.

"Don't worry," said Nanny Piggins. "I have a plan."

"Already?" exclaimed Michael, deeply impressed.

"Oh yes," said Nanny Piggins. "I can regale people with anecdotes from my sordid past and think at the same time."

Apparently, Nanny Piggins's plan involved going shopping because, without any further explanation, she ushered the children and Boris into Mr. Green's car (after getting the key out of Mr. Green's desk by forcing the lock with a sledgehammer) and drove off in the direction of the markets. Fortunately Mr. Green's car had a sun-roof, so even though he was ten feet tall, Boris was able to comfortably sit in the front seat. The suspension just sagged a bit on his side.

The markets were of the large, covered variety. There were hundreds of stalls selling everything from imported T-shirts, guaranteed to both shrink and fall apart the first time you wash them, to electronic games that only took the most inconvenient-sized batteries, to jellied eels. If it were not for the imminent kidnapping of their beloved nanny, the children would have enjoyed having a look around. But on this occasion they were not allowed that luxury.

"Spread out and start searching," Nanny Piggins instructed. "You'll be safe if you stay in pairs. Just remem-ber, if anyone tries to sell you overpriced handmade soap, don't make eye contact and walk away quickly."

"But what are we searching for?" asked Derrick.

"Trust me, you'll know," called Nanny Piggins as she disappeared behind a display of hideous tea towels.

Boris and the children looked at each other for a moment. "We'd better do as we're told," suggested Samantha.

And so they did. They split into two groups. Derrick searched with Samantha, and Boris searched with Michael. None of them had any idea what they were doing. But since this was so often the case, they were not particularly uncomfortable with the arrangement.

A short time later Michael and Boris had inadvertently wandered into the fresh-food section of the markets. Boris had unconsciously been drawn to the smell of honey-roasted peanuts, when they heard the sound of Nanny Piggins's voice.

"Get your broccoli here! Lots of healthy broccoli! If you don't want to die of bowel cancer, get your broccoli here!" called Nanny Piggins.

"That sounds like Nanny Piggins, but it doesn't sound like anything she would say," said Michael. He had never known his nanny to praise the health benefits of vegetables before.

"Let's go and have a look," said Boris.

So they walked toward the sound of Nanny Piggins's voice. She was saying more strangely uncharacteristic things, like, "Lots of lovely carrots! Good for your eyesight, even better for your bowels! Take them home tonight!"

Then, up ahead, they saw her. Nanny Piggins was standing in front of a stall and selling fruits and vegetables to passing shoppers.

"Sarah, what are you doing?!" exclaimed Boris, concerned that his sister had lost her mind.

Nanny Piggins looked Boris up and down. "I have no idea who you are," she said rudely, "but you're are very big and fat, so please move. You are blocking the view of my customers."

Boris promptly burst into tears. He was not really overweight. All bears are big-boned. Especially ones who are ten feet tall.

"Don't be mean to Boris," scolded Michael as he patted Boris's hand.

"You can run along as well. Children never buy fruits and vegetables. They always waste their money on chocolate," said Nanny Piggins contemptuously.

"Have you been hit on the head? Or suffered a stroke?" asked Michael, not meaning to be rude but genuinely concerned that something had gone wrong inside Nanny Piggins's brain. He had never known his nanny to be mean before.

"Suffered a stroke indeed! I've a good mind to give

you a stroke across the backside. Now clear off out of here!" said Nanny Piggins.

"Sarah Piggins! What's gotten into you?" wailed Boris. "Has stress driven you insane?"

"I have no idea what you are talking about. My name is not Sarah Piggins. I am Katerina Muellerstock. I've never known anyone called Sarah Piggins in my life. Except for my morally bankrupt twin sister, who works as a flying pig in the circus. And I shudder to think what has happened to her and her lower intestines by now, because she never ate any vegetables," said the pig.

"Oh come on, give it up, Nanny Piggins, there's no use pretending for us. We know you don't really have a twin sister," said Michael.

"What a rude little child you are. I bet you never eat any fruit, do you? You're probably older than you look because your growth has been stunted by a poor diet," she said.

Now Michael took exception to this. He was a little on the short side, but he rightly believed that was because he had been hit on the head by a falling dictionary as a small child.

"There's no need to be mean to the little one," argued Boris.

"He wouldn't be so little if he had more vitamins in his diet," she said.

Then, just as Boris drew breath to start yelling at her in Russian, their argument was interrupted.

"Katerina, we meet again," said a voice behind them.

Boris and the Michael turned to see... another Nanny Piggins standing right there.

"Aaahh!" screamed Boris because he was Russian and a ballet dancer, so he was twice as emotional as most bears. "One of them is a robot clone of Nanny Piggins! We'll never work out which is the real one."

Nanny Piggins (the one who had just arrived) stomped hard on Boris's foot.

"It's all right," said Boris immediately, calming down. "She's the real one. I'd know that stomp anywhere."

"Allow me to explain. Katerina is my identical twin sister," announced Nanny Piggins.

"You mean there *are* two of you?" exclaimed Michael.

"No," said Nanny Piggins. "There are fourteen of us."

Nanny Piggins took a crumpled old photograph out of her pocket and showed it to them. It was a picture of a very attractive-looking middle-aged pig, with fourteen identical baby piglets all crowded around her. "You see, there's me, there's Anthea, Beatrice, Abigail, Gretel, Deidre, Jeanette, Ursula, Charlotte, Wendy, Nadia, Sophia, Sue, and there's Katerina." Boris and the children stared hard at the photograph.

"But you all look exactly the same," pointed out Derrick.

"Of course we do," said the pig. "We're identical fourteentuplets. It's quite common in pigs, you know."

"Do we really have to have a family reunion in front of my stall on a market day?" asked Katerina rudely.

"Yes, we do," said Nanny Piggins. "Because I have a proposition to put to you."

.... ★ ★ ★ ....

Later that night, at exactly eight o'clock, the Ringmaster returned to the house. He did not bother to knock on the door. He climbed in through the upstairs bathroom window as a matter of course. But Samantha had been on the lookout so they were not at all surprised when he burst into the living room declaring, "Good evening!" In fact it was he who was surprised upon seeing Nanny

Piggins sitting next to her identical twin. "My goodness! Two flying pigs! I'm going to make a fortune!"

"No, you are not," said Nanny Piggins firmly. "You'll get just one flying pig and only if you agree to certain conditions."

"What conditions?" asked the Ringmaster.

"We'll get to those later. First of all I should explain. I am the real Sarah Piggins," said Nanny Piggins.

"I knew it," said the Ringmaster triumphantly.

"I shall not be returning with you. Partly because I have a much more important job looking after these children." Nanny Piggins smiled at the children. "But mainly because I don't want to. And you can't make me because I've consulted an astrologer and she assures me a contract signed by a three-year-old piglet is not legally binding."

"I don't see what's in this deal for me," said the Ringmaster, grumbling.

"I'm getting to that. I don't want to be a flying pig anymore. But my twin sister, Katerina Muellerstock, does," said Nanny Piggins.

"Really?" asked the Ringmaster, genuinely surprised, because he would never agree to be fired out of a cannon for all the money in Switzerland.

"But only…" continued Nanny Piggins, "…if you allow her the opportunity to educate the world about the benefits of eating vegetables."

"Are there any benefits?" Michael whispered to Boris. Boris just shrugged his shoulders.

"But how?" asked the Ringmaster.

"Katerina is willing to be fired out of a cannon and sent hurtling through the air in front of thousands of people on the condition that, as she does this, she can have a sign painted on her side saying, 'Eat more vegetables,'" explained Nanny Piggins.

"It is my motto, my mantra, and my life's work to spread this message," explained Katerina. "I am quite willing to risk my life to spread the word about the importance of a high-fiber diet."

"A flying pig with an important health message painted on her side," mused the Ringmaster. "That is bound to get a lot of publicity from the newspapers. I agree to it all!"

The Ringmaster and Nanny Piggins shook hands on it. Then the Ringmaster gave Katerina two kisses on each cheek. And then Katerina gave him a hard stomp on the foot. (Like Nanny Piggins, she had been raised properly.) This did not deter the Ringmaster at all. He was delighted by his feisty new flying star.

"I have a blank fifty-year contract here for you to sign," he said, holding out a contract and a pen to Katerina.

"There will be no more fifty-year contracts! Katerina will sign a one-year contract, with an option for renewal. But only on the condition that you present her with one thousand cabbages every second of October."

"I'd do anything for a nice cabbage," admitted Katerina.

So Katerina and the Ringmaster left happily together. Given his evil cunning and her puritanical meanness, they were well suited to each other. But, most important, Nanny Piggins, Boris, and the children were left in peace, without the immediate threat of being dragged anywhere, at least for the time being. So they all celebrated their good fortune with a big bowl of chocolates.

CHAPTER TEN

Nanny Piggins and the Great Pie Fiasco

amson Wallace's favorite thing in the world was to spend the day playing with the Green children, because their nanny, Nanny Piggins, would let them play his favorite game in the world: Mud People. Mud People was a game that involved digging a large pile of fresh dirt out of Mr. Green's rose bed, mixing it with water, then smearing it all over yourself and pretending to be a mud person.

Samson would never be allowed to play this at home. If he so much as got a speck of dust on his blazer he would get a stern talking-to from his own nanny, Nanny Anne.

Nanny Anne was perfect. She did everything perfectly, she said everything perfectly, and everything around her had to be perfect. If something was not perfect, she would not yell. She would sit you down and talk perfectly reasonably to you until you were so tired of her reasonableness that you lost the will to live.

The only reason Samson was able to play Mud People with the Green children was because Nanny Piggins had no qualms about deceiving Nanny Anne. Nanny Piggins simply provided Samson with a complete change of clothes (from Mr. Green's wardrobe) while he played the game. That way his own clothes could be taken and sealed in a plastic bag as soon as he entered the Green house and then returned to him in mint condition when they saw Nanny Anne walking up the front path.

On this particular day, when Nanny Anne reentered the house, she was almost disappointed to see that Samson's clothes were as immaculate as when she left him. (She had not figured out Nanny Piggins's plastic-bag trick.) She naturally suspected Nanny Piggins of subterfuge but she was too perfectly polite to say anything. Instead, her eyes searched for something to "compliment."

"Complimenting" things was Nanny Anne's way of insulting people. You see, if you insult people through compliments, by the time they figure out what you meant, you will have gone home so they cannot yell at you. For instance, Nanny Anne had, in the past, told Nanny Piggins that she "loved her hair. More people should be brave enough to try that unwashed look"; that she "loved her dress. It hid everything very well"; and that she "loved Nanny Piggins's cooking. It was fun to eat junk food every once in a while."

Unfortunately for Nanny Anne, on this particular day there was nothing to compliment. Nanny Piggins had thoroughly cleaned Samson with the garden hose, a scrubbing brush, and two liters of turpentine. So there was no moss behind his ears, lichen up his nose, or dirt under his fingernails, which was amazing given that only half an hour earlier, Derrick had dragged him backward through a bog.

But Nanny Anne had many more weapons at her disposal. After a lifetime of politely making other people feel inadequate and bad about themselves, she could not be bested so easily.

"Thank you so much for taking care of dear little Samson," began Nanny Anne.

"My pleasure," said Nanny Piggins, knowing her rival was up to something.

"We'll be seeing you at the competition tomorrow, then?" asked Nanny Anne.

"Yes, of course you will," agreed Nanny Piggins despite the fact that she had absolutely no idea what Nanny Anne was talking about.

Nanny Anne sensed that Nanny Piggins was bluffing. "You'll be entering then?" she asked.

This is where Nanny Piggins snapped. She was tired of trying to avoid being insulted. She just wanted this horrible nanny to leave her (Mr. Green's) house. "Entering what?" Nanny Piggins demanded. "A house? A doorway? A naval submarine? Would you please just specify what on earth you are talking about?"

Nanny Anne smiled smugly. She liked winning these little games. "Have you had too many sugary drinks, dear?" she asked reasonably. "You seem to be a little grumpy today."

Nanny Piggins hated it when Nanny Anne started using her reasonable voice on her; it made her want to bite the other nanny's leg. "Just tell me what it is you're talking about," said Nanny Piggins coldly.

Perhaps Nanny Anne sensed that she was about to be the victim of some terrible violence. Or perhaps, having won their mini-battle, she decided to put Nanny Piggins out of her misery. Either way she did explain herself. "The baking competition that's held every year at the town show. I was just wondering if you were planning to give it a go."

"Oh, that," said Nanny Piggins, trying to regain her dignity by pretending she had known about it all along. "Yes, I'm entering that. Of course, I am extremely busy. I have to test-fly a plane for NASA this weekend and discover a cure for pimples for Doctors Without Borders. But the mayor came to the house and personally begged me to participate. He said the quality of the competition had been so awful in previous years that they desperately wanted me to compete."

"I see," said Nanny Anne, for she was temporarily bested by this unexpectedly fictitious speech.

"You had better go now," said Nanny Piggins, opening the front door for Nanny Anne and Samson. "The children and I promised Greenpeace we would try to invent the hydrogen engine before dinner."

"Very well," said Nanny Anne. "I look forward to trying your pie."

Nanny Piggins was just in the process of slamming the door in Nanny Anne's face when she heard this last word and jammed her own hoof in the doorway, which hurt, but she did not care. "What did you say?" she demanded.

"I look forward to trying your pie," said Nanny Anne.

"Not cake?" asked Nanny Piggins hopefully.

"No, definitely pie. It is a pie-baking competition. Anyone can bake a cake, but a pie with a crust and a lid, that is a real cooking challenge." Nanny Anne was so satisfied with the deflated expression on Nanny Piggins's face, she turned on her heel and left.

Nanny Piggins closed the door and slumped down on the umbrella stand.

"What's wrong?" asked Michael. He had never seen his nanny looking so devastated before.

"Oh, children," said Nanny Piggins. "You had better fetch me some chocolate, I'm all aflutter." The children ran to the kitchen to fetch chocolate and they fetched Boris the bear from the garden shed too, because even though he was Russian and extremely overemotional, he was ten feet tall and children instinctively look to tall people for leadership.

"What's wrong?" asked Boris as they all watched Nanny Piggins wedge a large chocolate bar into her mouth.

"Oh, Boris," said Nanny Piggins between mouthfuls. "The most dreadful thing has happened. I am being forced to enter a pie-baking competition."

"No!" gasped Boris.

"Yes," admitted Nanny Piggins.

Boris wrapped Nanny Piggins in a big bear hug. "Don't worry, we'll help you through this."

"What's the problem?" asked Samantha. "Don't you know how to cook pie?"

Boris laughed once. "Ha!" This is the way people laugh in Russia when they want to be dramatic. "The problem is the exact opposite. Nanny Piggins is the greatest pie baker ever in the world."

"In the entire world?" asked Derrick. He was not exactly incredulous. But he was aware that the entire world was a large place.

"It's true," admitted Nanny Piggins, still chomping on the chocolate bar for comfort.

"But Nanny Piggins has never made a pie for us," Michael pointed out.

"Of course not," declared Boris. "She swore on her mother's snout that she would never bake another pie again."

"Why?" asked Samantha.

"Her pies were so good," whispered Boris, "they were dangerous!"

"How can a pie be dangerous?" asked Michael curiously. He had visions of exploding pies that he could take to school and give to his most horrible teacher.

"You'll soon find out. I'm going to start baking," said Nanny Piggins. She had finished her chocolate bar now.

"But you can't! You took an oath!" insisted Boris.

"I have to. It's a matter of pride. I have to do it to show Nanny Anne that she's a…she's a…she's a…" Nanny Piggins struggled to think just what Nanny Anne was.

"A big stupid head?" suggested Michael.

"That's exactly it," exclaimed Nanny Piggins. "Nanny Anne is a big stupid head and I refuse to let her show me up."

"But, Nanny Piggins," pleaded Boris, "you remember what happened last time."

"I was young and foolish then. I won't let that happen again," Nanny Piggins assured him.

"Well, I won't stand by and watch you do it," said Boris, drawing himself up to his full ten feet so that his head made a dent in the ceiling. "I refuse to support you. If you do this, I wash my hands of it!"

The children gasped. Boris did not often wash his hands so they knew this must be important.

"But, Boris, I hoped you'd help," said Nanny Piggins.

"I will have nothing to do with this terrible idea," said Boris, and with that he stomped out through the house, across the garden, into his shed, and slammed the door.

······· ★ ★ ★ ·······

Nanny Piggins enjoyed being lazy as much as the next person, but she was not afraid of hard work. The children had seen Nanny Piggins work hard many times: the time she carved a rude message into the side of Mr. Richardson's garage with a chain saw (a success), the time she made her own hang glider out of newspaper and Mr. Green's golf clubs (not a success), or the time she threw rock cakes at policemen to see if she could knock their hats off (a triumph). But they had never seen her work as hard as she did when she set to work baking pies.

Every part of the process was carried out meticulously. She stewed the filling, she mixed the pastry, and she prepared the baking dishes all with immaculate care. She approached the task with the concentration of a chess grand master. She did not joke about or juggle the utensils like she usually did when she was cooking.

Derrick, Samantha, and Michael did their best to help her while Nanny Piggins issued tense, whispered instructions, generally behaving as though she were defusing a bomb instead of making deliciously flaky short-crust pastry.

Once the pies (Nanny Piggins had made four pies "just in case") were in the oven, the children were relieved. They would be able to send a pie off to the competition and their nanny would go back to normal. They all sat and watched the pies baking through the glass oven door as though it were a television. They could see the pastry puff up and turn golden brown.

"How do you know when they are ready?" Michael asked.

Suddenly the oven made a *ping* noise.

"Because the oven will make a *ping* noise," declared Nanny Piggins, hopping off her seat and going over to the stove.

As she opened the oven door a delicious smell of buttery, apple-y goodness flooded out into the kitchen. The children breathed in deeply. It smelled heavenly. If there were a pie-smelling competition they were sure Nanny Piggins would have won already.

Nanny Piggins carried the hot pies over to the kitchen table.

"So, shall we pack one up and take it down to the town hall?" asked Samantha.

"In a minute. We'd better test one first, just to be sure," said Nanny Piggins.

This made sense to the children—after all, there were four pies. So they watched as Nanny Piggins cut a thin slice out of the pie and put in on a plate. Nanny Piggins then picked up a spoon, scooped up a small morsel, and blew on it, to cool it down. "Now for the moment of truth," she said before slipping the tiny piece of pie into her mouth. Then she closed her eyes and surrendered herself to the complete pie experience.

"How is it?" asked Derrick.

Nanny Piggins did not even open her eyes. "Mmm," she said.

"Is it good?" asked Michael. He was not fluent in "mmm" noises.

But Nanny Piggins still had her eyes closed. "Mmm-mm-mmm," she repeated.

"Are you all right?" asked Samantha, growing concerned that her Nanny was having a pie-induced out-of-body experience.

Nanny Piggins swallowed the pie and opened her eyes. "Poetry! A masterpiece! Breathtakingly beautiful!" she said. (When it came to her own pies, Nanny Piggins was not a modest pig.) There were tears in her eyes she was so emotional.

"It's good then?" queried Michael, just to confirm things.

"Well, that piece was," said Nanny Piggins. "But we will have to check the rest of the pie. It could have been a freak accident and only that tiny sliver was okay. We must check the other parts." So Nanny Piggins and the children picked up a spoon each and started testing the pie from all directions.

And the children had to admit, Nanny Piggins was not

exaggerating. The pie was "poetry," "a masterpiece," and "breathtakingly beautiful." If anything, she was understating the case. The children felt it was also "delicious" and "scrummy" as well as "yummy yummy yummy in their tummies." They checked all parts of the pie until it was all gone and they all agreed that every bit was excellent.

"You did it, Nanny Piggins! You made the perfect pie," said Derrick.

"I know. I told you I was the world's greatest pie baker," said Nanny Piggins, simply stating the facts.

"Now do we take one down to the town hall?" asked Samantha.

"I don't know," said Nanny Piggins cautiously. "Just because that pie was perfect does not mean the other three are. We had better check another one, just to be sure."

So Nanny Piggins and the children picked up their spoons and checked another pie. This second pie was just as good. It stood up to all their testing and soon there was nothing left but another empty plate.

"It wasn't an accident. You've made a perfect batch of pies," said Michael. He did not think it was possible that he could be more impressed with his nanny. He already knew she could fly out of cannons, scuba dive, and tap-dance.

But now that he knew she could bake pies better than anyone else in the world, he loved her even more.

"We've got two pies left and we only need one to enter the competition. So we might as well finish off the spare one," suggested Nanny Piggins. The children were happy to agree with this. You don't get to eat the world's best pie every day. So getting to eat three in a row was an opportunity too good to refuse. The third pie was soon gone.

They sat looking at the final competition-entry pie. It looked delicious. "You know," said Nanny Piggins. "It's sixteen hours until I have to enter the competition. If this pie was eaten, accidentally, somehow, there would still be plenty of time for me to make another one."

"I suppose," agreed Derrick. The pie did look very good. The children could see the sense in this so they all nodded their agreement.

"In fact, it would be much better if we ate this pie because sixteen hours is a long time for a pie to sit around. So if I made another pie that pie would be fresher," reasoned Nanny Piggins.

"That makes sense to me," said Michael.

"As long as it wouldn't be too much trouble," said Samantha.

"No trouble at all," Nanny Piggins assured her.

With that all four of them fell on the pie and gobbled it up greedily. They did not even bother to use spoons.

And so the night progressed. Nanny Piggins baked pie after pie, but then tested them all so rigorously that none of them lasted. The night wore on. By six o'clock in the morning, Derrick and Michael fell asleep, exhausted from helping Nanny Piggins "test" so many different pies— blackberry, blueberry, cherry, apple, apricot, chocolate cream, pecan, and pear, just to name a few.

Samantha was also exhausted. She had tried reasoning. She had tried arguing. She had even tried hiding a pie in the bread bin. But she could not stop Nanny Piggins from testing (eating) the pies as quickly as she made them. Something had to be done. Samantha did not want her beloved if somewhat pie-crazed nanny to be humiliated at the competition. So she snuck out of the kitchen and hurried across the garden to Boris's shed.

She knocked quietly on the door. Nothing happened. Then she remembered that Boris was a bear and you had to be less subtle with bears. So she broke into the shed and tipped a watering can full of water over his head.

"Is it time to get up already?" asked Boris as he wiped

the water out of his eyes. He did not mind at all that Samantha had been so forceful with him. In fact he liked it because it saved him having to take a shower later.

"Boris, you have to help," pleaded Samantha. "Nanny Piggins has become crazed with pie baking."

Boris shook his head sadly. "She's been eating her own pies, hasn't she?"

"That's exactly it!" exclaimed Samantha. "She eats every pie she makes. The entries have to be in by eight o'clock and it's six-thirty now. If she eats all of this batch she won't have time to bake another."

"Well, there's nothing I can do about that. I tried to warn her and she wouldn't listen," said Boris as he lay back down and started snoring to pretend he was asleep.

"Oh, Boris," said Samantha. "You aren't going to abandon Nanny Piggins just because she has been silly, vain, and greedy, are you? She's your sister. And it's times like these when you have completely lost your mind and eaten over fifty pies that you need your brother most."

Boris immediately burst into tears. He often did this because he was Russian and extremely in touch with his emotions. "You're completely right," wailed Boris, throwing his arms around Samantha in a big bear hug.

"I can't abandon my beloved sister just because she has gone pie crazy. I will come at once."

In the kitchen the morning sun was streaming in through the window. There were dirty dishes everywhere. At some point during the night Nanny Piggins had run out of pie dishes and started baking pies in butter dishes, teapots, jam jars, and even a goldfish bowl. (The goldfish was happily swimming in the toilet cistern and there was a big sign on the toilet saying DON'T FLUSH.)

When Boris and Samantha entered, Nanny Piggins was sitting at the end of the table. She looked exhausted. There was one final pie sitting in front of her. It was an apple and pear pie with raisins and a crisscross pastry crust. It was perfect. As the early morning sun lit up the room and shone on that perfect pie there was no doubt in Samantha's mind that her nanny had made the competition winner. But then she saw Nanny Piggins's face and the unmistakable look in her eye. Hunger.

"Don't do it," begged Samantha.

"I have to," said Nanny Piggins. She was practically weeping. "This is the perfect pie. With just the right amount of brown sugar, balsamic vinegar, and cinnamon to win over the judges."

"It's beautiful," Samantha agreed.

"That's just it," said Nanny Piggins. "I can't send this off to be eaten by strangers, heathens who don't appreciate the true beauty of a pie. The type of people who brush their teeth first so they can't taste anything. I can't do it. It wouldn't be fair to the pie!" And with that Nanny Piggins picked up her spoon.

"Stoooooop!!!" yelled Boris.

Nanny Piggins hesitated for just a fraction of a second. And Boris lunged toward her. Nanny Piggins desperately tried to take a scoop out of the pie, but she was knocked onto the floor by her thousand-pound brother.

Now Boris was ten feet tall and weighed one thousand pounds. Whereas Nanny Piggins was four foot two and ninety pounds. So as the two of them struggled— Boris trying to get the spoon away from her, and Nanny Piggins desperately trying to get back to the pie—you would think this would be an unequal wrestling match. But Nanny Piggins was an eighth-degree black belt in taekwondo and she liked to bite, which meant Boris had quite a fight on his hands.

Fortunately, Samantha was quick thinking. She grabbed the pie and ran. She ran with it into the living room,

Fortunately, Samantha was quick thinking.
She grabbed the pie and ran.

out the front door, down the garden path, and all the way down the street to the town hall. She ran as fast as she could, considering she was still in her nightdress, she wasn't wearing any shoes, and the pie dish was burning her hands. As Samantha turned the corner seven blocks away she could still hear Nanny Piggins's cries of "Nooooo! My pie! My pie!" echoing behind her.

★ ★ ★

A few hours later, Boris, the children, and Nanny Piggins made their appearance at the town show. Nanny Piggins was turned out very smartly in her Sunday best. But emotionally she was feeling fragile. She kept saying the same thing over and over again. "I'm so sorry. I don't know what came over me. I am so sorry."

Boris was very kindly holding her hand. "That's all right, Sarah, we know you have a problem with pies. But it's all over now."

"I will never bake or eat another pie for as long as I live," promised Nanny Piggins. "It's frightening the way I lose control."

The children hugged their nanny to show how much

they loved her. As far as personal problems go, being the world's greatest pie baker was a very pleasant problem for the friends of the sufferer. The children had quite enjoyed spending all night eating pie.

Unfortunately they could not avoid Nanny Anne. She was standing next to her own competition entry. It was a one-hundred-percent symmetrical low-fat pumpkin pie. (As you know, Nanny Piggins did not approve of putting any sort of vegetable even next to a pie, let alone in it.) Nanny Piggins grimaced as she looked at the pie with disgust. It was an unnatural orange color. There was not a single part of Nanny Piggins that felt like having a spoonful.

"Hello, Nanny Piggins," said Nanny Anne. "Do you like the look of my pie?"

"No, it looks disgusting. I'd rather eat my own hoof," said Nanny Piggins. When she wanted to insult a person, she just insulted them. Fortunately, before a fight broke out, Michael was able to change the subject.

"Oh look, Nanny Piggins," said Michael. "The judges are trying your pie now."

Nanny Piggins looked up to see three men wearing tweed jackets and a woman, who looked strangely like a horse, digging in to her pie. There was something about the sight of other people putting their spoons into Nanny Piggins's pie that made her brain snap, again.

Time seemed to stand still as an expression of pure hunger passed across Nanny Piggins's face. Then suddenly, she was galvanized into action.

"Noooooooo!!!!!" screamed Nanny Piggins as she ran forward and snatched up the pie. The next moment she was bursting out of the tent squealing, "It's mine, it's mine, it's mine…" running as fast as her hooves would carry her.

The judges chased after Nanny Piggins because they had only had one spoonful and the pie was so good they desperately wanted another. The children and Boris chased Nanny Piggins because they wanted to stop her before she had time to eat the pie. Nanny Anne chased the judges because she desperately wanted them to come back and say her pie was the best. And everybody else chased after them all to see what would happen next.

Sadly, nobody got to see what happened to the pie. After dodging around the Ferris wheel, through the fortune-teller's tent, and under the cotton candy cart, Nanny Piggins escaped her pursuers by climbing up a tree (which is not easy when you are carrying a pie). The leaves hid her from view. But everyone knew what she was doing. A pig eating a pie as fast as she can makes a very distinctive noise. When the gobbling and licking sounds finished, they knew it was all over because the empty pie dish fell out of the tree and clunked onto the grass below. The hungry judges were crestfallen and Nanny Anne was delighted.

★ ★ ★

Later that morning, after Boris and the children had coaxed Nanny Piggins out of her tree and wiped all the pie stains from her face, they went to watch the pie medal presentation ceremony. Nanny Piggins had been officially disqualified for stealing her own entry and destroying it before it could be conclusively judged. (The judges had wanted to test every last mouthful as well.) So the mayor hung the gold medal for pie baking around Nanny Anne's neck. Nanny Piggins heroically resisted the urge to pick up a handful of dirt and throw it at her.

The mayor gave a little speech about what a wonderful cook Nanny Anne was and what a joy it was to find a truly delicious low-fat alternative. It is amazing the lies men will tell to women when they are tall, blond, and beautiful. Nanny Piggins barely listened to a word he said until he got to the last sentence.

"And now that the pie-baking contest is over, we move on to the next stage — the pie-eating contest," said the mayor.

Nanny Piggins's ears instantly pricked up.

"If anybody would like to enter, just step forward now."

Nanny Piggins did not so much step up to the front table as leap in its general direction. A competition for eating pies sounded to her like the best idea for a competition ever. And she had done so much training, having eaten fifty-three pies just the night before.

As you can imagine, Nanny Piggins easily won the competition. The best her nearest rival managed was seventeen pies. Nanny Piggins managed sixty-eight. She could have eaten more. But they ran out. Well, they did not entirely run out. There was one pie left. The low-fat pumpkin pie made by Nanny Anne. But Nanny Piggins refused to eat anything low fat on the grounds that diet foods were disgusting.

So Nanny Piggins, Boris, and the children walked home very happy indeed. The children were happy because their nanny had yet again proved that she had skills greater than any other child-care worker. Boris was happy because, at the end of the day, his sister had vowed never ever to bake pies again. But best of all, Nanny Piggins was the happiest pig alive because her gold medal was one quarter of a millimeter larger than Nanny Anne's.

CHAPTER ELEVEN

Mr. Green's Evil Sister

r. Green liked making announcements at breakfast. It saved him having to spend extra time with his children. Nanny Piggins would have preferred it if he saved his news for just about any other part of the day. She thought mealtimes were sacred and that it was disrespectful to the food not to concentrate on stuffing as much of it in your mouth as possible. But she put up with Mr. Green's peculiar ways because she did not want to spend any extra time with him either.

On this particular morning, when Nanny Piggins heard Mr. Green folding up his paper and clearing his throat, she knew something was coming. So she quickly smeared a thick layer of jam over four slices of toast and stuffed them all in her mouth, just in case it was a long speech and she would need the extra energy to sit through it.

"I have an announcement to make," announced Mr. Green.

His children watched him warily. In their experience, announcements were never good, but just how not good they were could differ widely. Mr. Green always used the exact same tone of voice whether he was announcing that the lightbulb had blown in the downstairs bathroom, or announcing that their mother had just died in a mysterious boating accident. So they sat hoping that this time it was just a lightbulb. Sadly, it was something much, much worse than that.

"My sister, Lydia, is coming to stay," said Mr. Green.

Derrick and Samantha both managed to repress their instinct to groan. But Michael was the youngest and, therefore, the least able to control himself, so he burst out saying, "Oh no! Not that old—" before Samantha was able to silence him by shoving a muffin in his mouth.

Having started his announcement, Mr. Green had stopped listening (he was not a man who was good at multitasking), so he did not notice.

"You children are very lucky," went on Mr. Green. Which was always a sure sign that he was about to say something that would prove how deeply unlucky they were. You may have noticed that adults tell you that you should not lie. But then they have this strange habit of starting speeches by saying something that is the opposite of the truth. For example, whenever you hear someone say, "You'll be interested to hear…" or "Funnily enough…" or "With all due respect…" they always mean the exact reverse.

"Your aunt Lydia has decided to come and live with us," he announced to his horrified children and their equally horrified Nanny.

Now, just so you understand, there was absolutely no reason why Aunt Lydia should go to live with the Greens. When her husband died (coincidentally, he too had died in a mysterious boating accident) she had been left a wealthy widow. Not as rich as a pop star, but rich enough to own her own home, buy good food, and go to the movies whenever she liked. Which, as far as Nanny

Piggins and the children were concerned, was untold wealth.

Aunt Lydia and Mr. Green were very alike. Apart from having the same parents, and spouses that had died in exactly the same way, they were also alike in that they were both very cheap. They were miserly, penny-pinching skinflints. They never spent money if it could at all be avoided. They did not mind spending money on themselves to buy things like nice cars, clothes, and holidays, but anything else like bills, home maintenance, and food, they deeply begrudged. This is why Aunt Lydia wanted to come and live with Mr. Green. She did not like her brother and she certainly did not like his children, but she did like the idea of selling her house and having all that lovely money in a bank account earning interest. She also knew that if she lived in her brother's house he would have to pay all the electricity bills and buy all the food, which suited her very well.

The shocking thing was that Mr. Green had an ulterior motive too, which Nanny Piggins and the children were about to find out about.

"So, er... if she is staying here... um... obviously..." said Mr. Green, drawing his speech out as though he was afraid of the response the next sentence would create. (He had every reason to be afraid.) "If my sister is here we will no longer need a nanny."

At that moment Nanny Piggins and all three Green children gasped in horror. Derrick picked up his butter knife and wildly considered lunging at his father. Samantha tightly clutched either side of her dress because she did not know what her arms would do if she let them free, but she was sure it would be very bad for her father and the furnishings. And Michael loudly said a word that cannot be repeated in print.

Surprisingly, Nanny Piggins said nothing. She knew this was serious and when things get serious then it is time to start thinking before you speak. Her mind was racing through all the possible ways she could stop Mr. Green. Then all the ways she could get revenge on him for even thinking of it.

"Now, er...legally, Miss Piggins, I have to give you two weeks' notice," said Mr. Green. He had checked the law books the day before at work. He was surprised to learn that nannies had employment rights too. But legally they did and he would never dream of breaking the law unless he was certain he would get away with it. "So you will be staying on to help my sister, er..." (he struggled to think of a word here because he knew his sister did not like being helped with anything) "...to adjust to the household." Knowing full well his sister had never adjusted to anything in her life, and that life had always been adjusted to suit her.

Mr. Green looked about him to see the effects of his announcement. His oldest son was clutching a butter knife and glaring at him in the most unnerving manner. His daughter's face had gone bright red as though she had been holding her breath for fear that opening her mouth would cause her to scream. And his youngest son was muttering very bad words, which he could only assume the boy had picked up from watching late-night television.

The most frightening sight was, however, the glare being given to him by the nanny. Her look was so mean and intense he could have sworn she was trying to put some kind of ancient voodoo curse on him. (And indeed she was.)

Mr. Green conveniently decided that he had better go to work. "Your aunt Lydia shall arrive in about twenty minutes," said Mr. Green as he looked at his watch. "I trust you shall make her welcome." With that he positively ran out of the room.

Neither Nanny Piggins nor the children said anything for a full minute as they each privately tried to contain their rage. It was Nanny Piggins who spoke first.

"Children, I know I should not speak ill of your father in front of you. But I am afraid one thing has to be said. He is a very, very bad man." And that was it. She had opened the floodgates. The four of them spent the next fifteen minutes screaming abuse about Mr. Green. By the time they had finished they had done absolutely nothing to solve the problem but they all felt a whole lot better, having had a good scream about it.

"What are we going to do?" despaired Derrick.

"You can't leave us, you just can't!" whimpered Samantha. She was clearly on the verge of bursting into tears.

"Can we all run away? Please, Nanny Piggins, please," begged Michael politely. He was always at his most polite when he desperately wanted something. (But then, aren't we all?)

"Now, children, it is very important we don't panic," said Nanny Piggins as she struggled not to panic. "I have no intention of leaving you." Apart from the fact that

Nanny Piggins liked how well stocked Mr. Green always kept his cupboards, she had also grown very attached to the children. The thought of leaving them made her stomach go all hard and her eyes feel itchy. Nanny Piggins was not a pig given to fits of hysterics or collapsing and crying on the tablecloth, but she knew she was seriously upset because she actually regretted eating eleven muffins for breakfast. "We mustn't do anything rash. We have two weeks to get rid of your aunt and disabuse your father of this ridiculous idea. We must handle this strategically and wisely."

And at that exact moment the doorbell rang.

"Crikey, she's here!" exclaimed Michael.

"Should we hide under the table?" asked Samantha hopefully.

"We could just not let her in," thought Nanny Piggins out loud, seeing no reason why they should not start making the aunt unwelcome from the start.

But then they heard the unfortunate sound of a key in a lock. Mr. Green had obviously given his sister her own key.

"We're doomed," said Derrick. The others silently agreed with him.

"What are we going to do?" asked Samantha, turning to Nanny Piggins for reassurance.

Nanny Piggins had not figured out a whole plan yet but she did need a first tactic. She knew that it was traditional for children to be very mean and beastly to child-care workers they did not like. That is what always happened in books. So she decided they should take the opposite tactic. "We are going to be incredibly nice and polite to your aunt," declared Nanny Piggins.

"But why?" asked Michael.

"If she is anything like your father, having people be nice to her will be a new experience and she won't know how to cope with it," said Nanny Piggins. "That should buy us time to come up with a plan."

★ ★ ★

As it turned out, Aunt Lydia was even more unpleasant than Mr. Green. She was very mean to Nanny Piggins. She seemed to think it was unusual to let a pig sleep in the house, and she was not at all impressed that Nanny Piggins was a circus star.

Aunt Lydia was also extremely unpleasant to the

children. One day when they were in the garden playing, she burned all their clothes in the fireplace, then forced them to wear clothes she had handmade herself out of wool. Now wool can be very itchy at the best of times. But the clothes Aunt Lydia made were so itchy the children were sure she had put itching powder in them as well, just to be spiteful.

But poor Boris suffered the most. Unlike Mr. Green, Aunt Lydia actually did like gardening. It gave her an excuse to hang around the backyard spying on the neighbors. So Boris had to hide himself in the compost heap every time Aunt Lydia went into the shed looking for garden tools, which was quite a lot. And if you have ever tried hiding in a compost heap, you will know it is extremely unpleasant. For a start, rotting vegetables are surprisingly hot. Then there is the smell, which is disgusting, even to a bear who does not have great body odor in the first place.

The tactic of being polite to Aunt Lydia did not work at all. She assumed that any child who said "please," "thank you," or "excuse me" was simply being sarcastic. So politeness was met with exactly the same punishment as rudeness.

And Aunt Lydia had such strange ideas about disciplining children. To make them cleverer she would make them do their homework (which, in Nanny Piggins's opinion, was inhumane in itself). But then when the children finished their schoolwork Aunt Lydia would set fire to it and make them do it all again.[3]

Arson was Aunt Lydia's answer to a lot of things. When Nanny Piggins went to answer the phone one day, she returned to the kitchen to find her chocolate cake on fire. Aunt Lydia did it to teach her a lesson about not talking for too long on the telephone. Nanny Piggins had spent twenty-five seconds on the phone, which in Aunt Lydia's opinion was twenty-three seconds too long.

Mr. Green did not escape Aunt Lydia's sense of discipline either. She set fire to his neckties if she did not like them. She also set fire to his theater ticket (he only had one because no one would go with him) when she wanted him to stay home and hand wash her socks. Aunt Lydia's

---

[3] Now reader, setting fire to things is obviously terrible, wrong, and incredibly dangerous. It just goes to show how deeply unpleasant Aunt Lydia was that she did not heed those very wise television commercials that remind us all never to play with fire.

personal motto was "All life's problems can be solved with dry kindling and a match." She had embroidered this on a wall hanging that she hung in her bedroom.

"Hasn't anybody ever told Aunt Lydia it is wrong to play with matches?" asked Nanny Piggins.

"I don't think anyone tells Aunt Lydia anything. She's too scary," explained Samantha.

By the end of the first week, they were all exhausted from being tortured. "Sarah, you have to do something," begged Boris as he, the children, and Nanny Piggins sat hidden behind a large bush in the garden, sucking the chocolate off chocolate-covered oranges.

"I know, but I can't figure out what," said Nanny Piggins. No one wanted to get rid of Aunt Lydia more than she. She did not like the glint in Aunt Lydia's eye every time she said, "A pig's place is between two slices of bread in a bacon sandwich," which she managed to bring up in conversation quite a lot.

"Couldn't we put her in a crate and ship her off to Russia?" suggested Michael. He knew that Boris had arrived in a crate from Russia so he assumed you could ship a crate the other way.

"You couldn't do that to the Russians," protested Boris. "They've suffered enough. First communism, then your aunt — it would be too much for them."

"I think Michael is on to something. There must be somewhere we could send her," pondered Nanny Piggins.

At that moment they were disturbed by a hideous noise.

"What on earth is that?!" exclaimed Nanny Piggins, almost spitting out her chocolate-covered orange. "It sounds like someone is murdering a cat in a blender."

"Or running over a set of bagpipes with a lawn mower," said Boris.

"Or torturing a hyena with an electric pencil sharpener," said Derrick.

"I know what it is," said Samantha. "It's Aunt Lydia singing!"

"No!" exclaimed Nanny Piggins. "Surely not?"

They all peered around the bush they were hiding behind to have a look. And sure enough, there was Aunt Lydia kneeling in front of the border (weeding it for the seventh time that week) and opening and closing her mouth in the manner of somebody singing, even though the noise coming out of her mouth bore no resemblance to singing whatsoever.

It was horrible, tuneless, and discordant, not unlike the sound of a piano accordion being chopped up with an axe.

The children and Boris hastily picked up the pieces of orange they had spat out and stuffed them in their ears to try to block out the sound. But Nanny Piggins kept watching in awed fascination. She was beginning to get a brilliant idea.

Aunt Lydia finally got to the end of her "song" and as soon as she finished her last quavering note she was greeted by the sound of clapping. Nanny Piggins was standing three feet away, applauding.

"Bravo, Aunt Lydia, that was beautiful. I am moved to tears," said Nanny Piggins, dabbing her completely dry eyes. "I never knew you had such a lovely singing voice!"

"Oh," said Aunt Lydia, somewhat taken aback. Unsurprisingly, she had never been complimented on the quality of her singing before. People usually commented on the power of her voice, or the piercing sound, or how far the noise carried. "I have been singing with the church choir for forty years," she said modestly.

"What a joy you must bring to your choirmaster's heart," said Nanny Piggins rapturously, for she was a very good actress.

"Actually, we have had forty-one different choirmasters in those forty years," admitted Aunt Lydia.

They had all been driven away by the sound of Aunt Lydia's voice as soon as their one-year contract had expired. One choirmaster had even been driven away *before* his contract expired when Aunt Lydia had caught him in his office and treated him to her solo rendition of "Ave Maria." He was now living in a cave in the mountains where he would never have to hear singing again.

"But they were all most impressed with my voice," boasted Aunt Lydia, which was true. They had all sat down in shock and dabbed their foreheads with handkerchiefs, saying things like, "Oh my goodness!" "What a voice!" and "What am I going to do with you?"

"But surely you have been besieged with offers to sing professionally at opera houses and to record albums of your greatest hits?" asked Nanny Piggins.

"Well no," admitted Aunt Lydia. While she was very cruel, she was also truthful.

"We have to do something about that," declared Nanny

Piggins. "It is unfair to the world of music for your talent to be squandered here in Mr. Green's backyard."

"Do you really think so?" asked Aunt Lydia, because even though she was horrible, she was a woman, and all women secretly, or not so secretly, want to be beloved singing sensations.

"I don't think so — I know so," Nanny Piggins assured her. "I have a dear friend who is a singing talent scout. He travels the world finding the greatest singers and offering them places at his exclusive singing school in Europe."

Aunt Lydia was practically drooling at the prospect of meeting such a man.

"Please, please say you will let me introduce him to you!" begged Nanny Piggins.

"All right, I will," said Aunt Lydia, thinking to herself that she had misjudged this pig and that Nanny Piggins was by far the most intelligent pig she had ever met.

.... ★ ★ ★ ....

Later that evening Aunt Lydia was sitting in the living room wearing her starchiest, ugliest gray dress and awaiting the arrival of Nanny Piggins's friend.

"What are you going to do, Nanny Piggins?" asked Derrick. "Do you really know a great European singing maestro?"

"And is he really coming to the house?" asked Samantha.

"And is he brain damaged enough to think Aunt Lydia can sing?" asked Michael.

"You'll just have to wait and see for yourselves," whispered Nanny Piggins smugly. She was clearly up to something because she kept winking and grinning gleefully.

Aunt Lydia did not like to admit she was nervous but she obviously was because she kept sipping from her teacup even though nothing had been put in it. When the doorbell rang she jumped up before she remembered that she was a dignified lady who should be sitting up straight and scowling.

"I'll get the door, shall I?" suggested Nanny Piggins.

"Thank you, Nanny Piggins, that would be most kind," said Aunt Lydia, and she practiced being even more stiff and formal than usual so as to impress her visitor.

Nanny Piggins disappeared from the room and returned just few moments later.

"May I introduce Professor Ludwig Von Buellerhousen

"May I introduce Professor Ludwig Von Buellerhousen of the Lapland Philharmonic Choir," announced Nanny Piggins.

of the Lapland Philharmonic Choir," announced Nanny Piggins. Then she bowed low as the professor himself entered the room.

The children held their breath in anticipation and were delighted to see that Professor Von Buellerhousen was none other than Boris wearing a monocle and a flowing black cape.

"Why, that's just Bo—" Michael blurted out before Samantha was able to silence him by stuffing a cupcake in his mouth.

"Good evening, I am a very busy and important man," said Boris. Nanny Piggins had instructed him to say this because it is always sensible to tell people what to think of you, in case they are too dim-witted to figure it out for themselves. "But I rushed to this abode when I heard that a great new singing talent had been discovered here. Where is this vocal prodigy?" he asked as he adjusted his monocle and peered about the room.

"Professor Von Buellerhousen, the prodigy you speak of is I," said Aunt Lydia awkwardly. It's hard not to sound like an idiot when that is what you are trying so desperately not to do.

"You!" exclaimed Professor Von Buellerhousen (who,

don't forget, was really just Boris). "But you are so beautiful!" Now he was, of course, lying here. And we all know lying is wrong. But it's okay if you lie to really wicked people. "Surely you cannot have both beauty and talent!" He was really laying it on thick but people are always prepared to believe untruths when they are about how wonderful they are.

Nanny Piggins thought she had better intervene here to move things along. "It is true, just wait until you hear her sing — it will make your hair stand on end," said Nanny Piggins. Strictly speaking, this was entirely accurate. Aunt Lydia's voice did make your hair stand on end, just not in a good way. Rather the way it does if you hear someone scrape her fingernails down a blackboard.

"If you will do me the honor, madam, nothing could bring me greater pleasure," said Boris as he helped himself to a cupcake. If he was about to hear something awful he needed a bit of cake to fortify himself.

"All right," agreed Aunt Lydia. "If you insist." She stood up, took a deep breath, and burst into song. The noise was every bit as awful as the noise she had made in the garden. If anything, it was worse because she was singing louder to impress Boris.

"Stop!!!" yelled Boris. "I don't need to hear any more." (Which was certainly true.) "I must immediately send you to my school for brilliant singers in Lapland. I will not take no for an answer. It is a crime for a voice such as yours to go unheard."

"Well, I don't know. I have made a commitment to my brother," said Aunt Lydia, looking around at the three children she detested. "Where is this school exactly?"

"In Lapland. All the best singers come from Lapland," declared Boris.

"They do?" asked Aunt Lydia.

"Oh yes, Pavarotti, Caruso, Dolly Parton—all proud Laplanders. And you are so talented you must have the very best teachers working with you."

"Well, if you insist," said Aunt Lydia. She did not need much persuading.

"I insist!" declared Boris.

"But how shall I get to Lapland?" asked Aunt Lydia.

"I have your means of transport waiting directly outside," said Boris.

"You do?" said Aunt Lydia.

"I had a premonition I would be meeting genius tonight," Boris assured her.

How could Aunt Lydia say no to that? She could not. Which is why she said yes, and within five minutes she found herself nailed into a large, bear-sized circus crate and on a ship to Lapland.

★ ★ ★

"But when she gets to Lapland, what if she decides to come back?" worried Samantha later that night.

"Don't worry about it," Nanny Piggins assured her. "That is all taken care of. My friend Lars was having trouble keeping the wolves away from his reindeer. He is going to use your aunt's singing to frighten them off."

"But won't Aunt Lydia figure it out?" asked Derrick skeptically.

"I shouldn't think so," said Nanny Piggins. "She is very nasty but not a particularly clever lady. And I've told Lars to wear a black cape and a monocle, and to tell her that singing outside in the snow will be good for her voice. It should be years before she works it out."

"But won't Father be angry when he finds out Aunt Lydia has gone?" asked Michael.

"I'll tell you what," said Nanny Piggins. "Let's play a

game. Let's play the How Long Will It Take Mr. Green to Realize His Sister Isn't Here Game."

As it turns out, it was a very good game. It was fascinating to see Mr. Green overlook all the obvious clues of his sister's absence—such as her not being there at breakfast, her not being there at lunch, and her not being there at dinner. It took him sixteen days to notice she was gone. Then, for another three days, Nanny Piggins managed to convince him that she had just popped out to the store for milk.

By the time Mr. Green realized that his sister had been missing for three weeks, he felt a bit sheepish about it. So he decided to not ask any questions, since that was the easiest thing to do. This meant that Nanny Piggins, the children, and Boris were able to go back to enjoying their everyday lives without the supervision of a responsible adult, which was just the way they liked it.

And so, even though Mr. Green had only hired her for a few days, Nanny Piggins had spent nearly a full year in the Green house. She and Boris had become part of the family, much more so than Mr. Green himself. And, for the first time in their lives, Derrick, Samantha, and

Michael woke up every morning feeling happy. They did not know what sort of adventure they would have that day. But when your nanny is a flying pig, you can be sure your next adventure will be starting soon ... possibly even before breakfast.

ACKNOWLEDGMENTS

I would especially like to thank...

Mum & Dad

Elizabeth Troyeur

Esther Perrins

Linsay Knight

Chris Kunz

Connie Hsu

and

Secretary Madeleine Albright

Turn the page for a sneak peek at Nanny Piggins's next amazing, high-flying, chocolaty adventures in *Nanny Piggins and the Wicked Plan*!

Nanny Piggins and the Tunnel to China

It all started with Nanny Piggins reading the most brilliant pirate story ever. She became so absorbed in the book that she could not put it down, not even for meals. Derrick, Samantha, and Michael had to feed Nanny Piggins snacks while she kept her eyes glued to the pages. The only time she took a break was at the end of each chapter so she could act it all out for the children and Boris. They loved this bit.

Nanny Piggins was very good at acting out novels. She did all the voices, all the silly walks, and all her own stunts. Her demonstration of Captain Bad Beard's attack of the *Good Ship Lollipop* was spectacular. It involved swinging from the living room chandelier with a spatula between her teeth before savaging her imaginary enemy. (Suffice to say, Mr. Green's ottoman would never be the same again.) So when Nanny Piggins finished the pirate book, they were all very sad.

"I wish we were pirates," said Nanny Piggins wistfully. "Pirate life has so much going for it: battles, seafood, and, best of all, treasure."

"It's almost as glamorous a job as being a nanny," said Boris.

"I know," agreed Nanny Piggins. "You children should really consider piracy. Do they ever ask pirates to come and speak to you at your school's career day?"

"No," admitted Derrick. "They usually just have accountants come and tell us how accountancy is really exciting."

"They let people come and lie to you?" asked Nanny Piggins. "Your headmaster is a very immoral man. Still, I suppose you don't need career advice to become a pirate—you just run away to sea."

"But the truancy officer gets upset when we don't

go to school," said Michael. "So I'm sure she'd get really upset if we ran away to live a life of crime on the high seas."

"She's such a spoilsport," sighed Nanny Piggins. (Nanny Piggins did not think much of the truancy officer. She was diabetic, so Nanny Piggins could not bribe her with cake.) "I'm sure you'd learn more as a pirate. After all, pirates need to know how to sew sails, tie knots, and blast cannons at passing ships. Now that's much more practical than that 'math'"—Nanny Piggins always said *math* as though it were a swear word—"they insist on teaching you at school."

"And, I bet they don't have to wash every day," mused Derrick. "Nanny Piggins is right. We should become pirates!"

"What?!" worried Samantha. After all, she was a shy girl. She did not like talking to strangers, let alone attacking them on the open ocean.

"We all have to get jobs eventually, so why not take up piracy now?" he continued.

"We'd learn lots of geography, oceanography, and the importance of avoiding scurvy," piped up Michael.

"And I really like those puffy shirts pirates wear," added Boris.

"Then that's decided. We're all becoming pirates. What do we do first?" asked Derrick.

"We need treasure," declared Nanny Piggins.

"But where are we going to find treasure?" asked Michael. "Father doesn't even give us pocket money, so he's never going to give us treasure."

"Treasure isn't something you get given," explained Nanny Piggins. "It's something you dig up. It's always buried."

"Why?" asked Samantha. It was bad enough she was becoming a pirate, but now it seemed she was doomed to have dirty fingernails as well.

"Because pirates never open bank accounts. They don't like filling out forms," said Nanny Piggins.

"But where are we going to find buried treasure?" asked Michael.

"In the ground, of course," said Nanny Piggins patiently. "There's probably lots buried in the back garden right now."

"Really?" said Derrick.

"There's only one way to find out," said Nanny Piggins.

And so Nanny Piggins rang the school and said that all three Green children had been struck down with a case of twenty-four-hour smallpox. Then they set to work being pirates. The first thing they needed was the right clothes, so Nanny Piggins took them up to Mr. Green's bedroom and plundered his wardrobe. He had very boring clothes, but with some dye, permanent markers, a pair of scissors, and a sewing machine, Nanny Piggins was soon able to turn one of Mr. Green's best suits into five excellent pirate costumes.

Then they went out into the garden with their spades.

"Where do we start?" asked Derrick as he looked around his father's garden for a likely spot.

"In pirate stories, X always marks the spot," reasoned Nanny Piggins. "So the first thing we shall have to do is make an X, then dig beneath it!"

And that is exactly what they did. Nanny Piggins marked an X right in the middle of Mr. Green's perfectly tended lawn, then immediately started hacking up the turf with her spade.

It soon became clear that Nanny Piggins was really good at digging for treasure. Thanks to all the cake she ate, she had boundless energy. Once the spade was in her trotters, she just dug and dug and dug. The children tried to help, but they could not keep up. And Boris kept shrieking and jumping out of the hole every time he saw a worm. So Nanny Piggins put them all in charge of supplies (fetching cake) and keeping watch for enemy pirates (the truancy officer), and that arrangement worked well.

By midmorning Nanny Piggins had dug a very, very deep hole—so deep she could not climb out of it. The children had to make a rope ladder out of Mr. Green's neckties to get her out in time for morning tea.

As they sat in the sun and ate their chocolate chip cookies, Nanny Piggins, Boris, and the children were very happy. Being pirates had been very satisfying so far. Really, there was just one problem. "You haven't had much luck finding treasure," Michael politely pointed out. They all looked at the small pile of things Nanny Piggins had found in her hole. It consisted of three buttons, a spoon, an apple core, a Frisbee, and the handle from a teacup.

"What are you talking about?" protested Nanny Piggins. "I've found three buttons! They'll be invaluable next time your trousers start falling down."

"But you haven't found a chest full of gold and jewels," pointed out Derrick. "That's what pirates always look for in books."

"I suppose," conceded Nanny Piggins, who, nevertheless, still felt proud of her buttons.

"Why don't you try digging somewhere else?" suggested Derrick, hopeful that they might get the next day off school as well.

"Well, it seems a shame when this is such a good hole," said Nanny Piggins. "I might as well keep going with this one."

"Why?" asked Samantha. She liked a hole as much as the next girl, but it seemed to her that it was plenty big enough.

"I'm starting to get peckish," explained Nanny Piggins, "so I thought I'd keep digging all the way through the center of the world until I end up in China. Do you fancy some Chinese food?"

The Green children loved Chinese food, so they agreed this sounded like an excellent plan. (They had set out for Chinese food some months ago, but high seas and colliding with a Korean fishing boat had delayed them.) The children were not entirely sure whether burrowing through the center of the earth was the quickest way to get to China. But China was certainly a long way away, and the earth was round. So through the ground was undeniably the shortest route.

Nanny Piggins finished her morning tea and kept on digging. She dug and dug and dug, for day after day. Although not all in a straight line. After day two she found it too hard to keep digging straight down because there was too much rock in the way. So Nanny Piggins started digging sideways instead.

On day three, the truancy officer came and dragged the children back to school. Apparently you are not allowed to quit school and become a pirate until you are sixteen, even if you do have a signed permission slip from your nanny.

And on day four, Boris had to go because he had promised to teach ballet to vagrants down at the YMCA.

So Nanny Piggins had to continue with her hole alone. Until, suddenly, on the eighth day of digging, her spade hit a piece of stone that gave way, and on the other side she could see a light. Nanny Piggins was very excited. A light could mean only one thing—she had tunneled all the way through to China!

Nanny Piggins hacked more rock out of the way to make the hole bigger, then wriggled out through the opening into the foreign and exotic land. But when she looked about, Nanny Piggins was startled to discover that China was not at all how she'd expected it to be. She was expecting a great big country with Chinese restaurants in every direction as far as the eye could see. In reality, China was just a very large room with forty men all hanging around, playing cards, and lifting weights.

"Hello," said Nanny Piggins, because she had forgotten to learn Chinese. Fortunately the Chinese men seemed to understand English, because they all looked up and stared at her. They were naturally surprised to find a filthy pig dressed as a pirate suddenly arriving in their country.

"What do you want?" asked the biggest and scariest of the men as he stood up and loomed over Nanny Piggins.

"Oh good, you speak English," said Nanny Piggins. "Could I have some Chinese food please?" She was not at all scared. She was prepared to pay for the food. She had found two quarters down the back of Mr. Green's couch just the other day.

"What?" demanded the scary-looking man in a very unfriendly manner.

Nanny Piggins looked around. He was not the only man in the room who looked unfriendly. Most of the men were frowning, some were scowling, and one man in the corner was nervously biting his nails. They all looked unhappy. Nanny Piggins could see these men needed help. Luckily, being a circus pig, she knew just how to cheer them up — with a show!

And that is just what she gave them. After three hours of her best tap dancing, followed by knife juggling and fire breathing, the men were delighted. They were calling for more. They even sent someone to the kitchen to whip up some chow mein for her, so she would have enough energy for an encore.

Many hours later, Nanny Piggins returned to the Green house with wonderful stories about the hospitality of the men in China.

Derrick and Samantha were naturally suspicious. They knew their nanny was an amazing woman. And they were sure that she was capable of tunneling much farther than any other nanny. But they had studied some geography at school, so they were not entirely convinced that even Nanny Piggins could dig all the way through the center of the earth to China in just eight days.

"Are you absolutely sure it was China?" worried Samantha. (She was not sure what to worry about, but the situation was making her feel a general, all-purpose worry.)

"Of course," said Nanny Piggins.

"Did it look like China?" asked Derrick excitedly.

"What does China look like?" asked Nanny Piggins, because pigs are lucky enough to not be forced to study geography.

"Did you see the Great Wall of China, the Entombed Warriors, Tiananmen Square, or anything like that?" asked Samantha.

"Did they have dim sum?" asked Michael, knowing that his nanny was more likely to have noticed food.

"I didn't see any of those things. But there was a big gray room with lots of men in it," said Nanny Piggins.

"I suppose that could be China," conceded Samantha. "They have gray rooms and men in most countries."

"Why don't you come and see for yourselves tomorrow?" suggested Nanny Piggins. "After all, it will be a wonderful educational opportunity for you to experience a different culture, and going to school one day a week should be more than enough to satisfy the truancy officer."

"Would we need to take our passports?" asked Samantha.

"Do you have passports?" asked Nanny Piggins.

"No," admitted Derrick.

"Then you'd better not bring them," reasoned Nanny Piggins.

······································ ★ ★ ★ ·······································

At ten o'clock the next morning, Nanny Piggins rang the school and said that Derrick, Samantha, and Michael had come down with twenty-four-hour bubonic plague. Then they all climbed down into the tunnel and set out for China.

On emerging from the other end of the hole, it became immediately clear to the Green children that there was, indeed, no need for passports. Because they were not in China. They were in a maximum-security prison.

"We're going to be in so much trouble," wheezed Samantha as she started to hyperventilate. She had suspected that Nanny Piggins would land them all in jail one day. But she had thought it would be through doing something wrong, not through digging a tunnel and voluntarily climbing in.

"What are you talking about?" Nanny Piggins was puzzled. "We're in China. Why would we be in trouble?"

"This isn't China," explained Derrick.

"Are you sure?" asked Nanny Piggins. "I ate some lovely chow mein here yesterday."

"This is a prison," explained Michael.

"A what-son?" asked Nanny Piggins.

"A place where the government locks up bad men," explained Michael.

"They lock up bad men?" asked Nanny Piggins. This took her by surprise. In her opinion the government had the most peculiar ways of doing things.

"Yes, people who steal or cheat on their taxes or hurt other people get locked up," explained Michael.

"Then why isn't your father in prison?" asked Nanny Piggins.

The children had to think for a moment. It was a good question.

"Because he's never been caught," suggested Derrick.

"Prison seems like a very drawn-out way of punishing people. When I'm cross with someone, I just bite them on the leg. And if I'm really cross, I bite them on both legs," said Nanny Piggins. Not that she needed to tell the children. They had seen the teeth scars on their father's calves. (Unlike the government, she had caught him many times.)

"Are you going to tap dance for us again, Nanny Piggins?" asked Phillip, who was serving two years for stealing his grandmother's wheelchair and taking it for a joyride.

"No, you were such good hosts last time I visited, I just popped in to see if you'd like to share morning tea at our home," said Nanny Piggins with her most gracious hostess smile.

"What?!!!" exploded Derrick and Samantha.

Michael did not say anything. He was too busy rushing back up the tunnel to hide his teddy bear.

"You can't invite them over," said Samantha with some difficulty because she was trying to talk out of the side of her mouth while still smiling at the men.

"Why not?" asked Nanny Piggins.

"Because they're prisoners. They aren't allowed to leave," explained Derrick.

"Piffle. I'm sure no one will mind if we bend the rules a little," said Nanny Piggins.

"But that's the whole point of prison. You have to stay in no matter what," said Samantha.

"Even if there's a half-price chocolate sale at the supermarket?" asked Nanny Piggins.

"Even then," confirmed Derrick.

"They must be very wicked men to get such harsh punishment," marveled Nanny Piggins. "Still, it's important to be polite. Always remember, children, there is no greater crime than rudeness. They hosted me, so I must invite them over." Nanny Piggins turned and loudly addressed all the men. "Would you all like to come and visit us for morning tea?"

"Yes, please!" said all the prisoners.

"Nanny Piggins!" exclaimed Derrick.

"They're prisoners," pleaded Samantha.

"You'll promise to come back here again afterward, won't you?" asked Nanny Piggins.

"Of course," said the prisoners.

"But the guards will notice that they're gone," argued Samantha.

"That's okay. We'll leave a note letting the guards know where we are," said Nanny Piggins. "They can't complain about that."

Derrick and Samantha suspected that the guards could indeed complain about that, but there was no time to discuss it further. Nanny Piggins was already shepherding prisoners into the tunnel ahead of her and telling them to put the kettle on when they got to the house so she could make them some hot chocolate.